Henry B. James

Memories of the Civil War

Henry B. James

Memories of the Civil War

ISBN/EAN: 9783337220914

Printed in Europe, USA, Canada, Australia, Japan

Cover: Foto ©Andreas Hilbeck / pixelio.de

More available books at **www.hansebooks.com**

MEMORIES OF
THE CIVIL WAR.

BY

Henry B. James,

✻ Co. B, 32nd Mass. Volunteers. ✻

"To you my comrades whether far or near,
I send this message, let our past revive;
Come, sound reveille to our hearts once more."

NEW BEDFORD, MASS.
FRANKLIN E. JAMES.
1898

To my Boys,

*Who delighted in their childhood
to hear their father tell stories of
the war, and at whose desire these
memories have been recalled, this
book is*

— DEDICATED. —

PREFACE.

I have written this account of my experience in the service of my country from memory, aided by old diaries, letters, etc., and have endeavored to be as accurate as possible, in regard to dates and events of historical importance, but if mistakes occur, it cannot be wondered at, after such a lapse of time. Some of my diaries were lost upon the battlefield, and of those that remain, many of the entries were in pencil and are almost effaced.

I had no intention when I began writing of making a long story, but as I went on, memory brought back many a stirring scene, many a weary march, many a tender thought of comrades who shared them all with me, and so I have written them down as they came to me.

My thanks are due my wife for so carefully editing, and my son for printing my attempt to keep in a permanent form, my recollections of the War of the Rebellion.

Chapter I.

ENLISTMENT.

To Arms! To Arms! Our country calls for aid,
Of faithful sons an offering must be made.
From every hamlet in the loyal North,
Her sturdy yeomen in their strength go forth;
Mechanics, merchants, all professions too,
Give up the arts of peace, another to pursue.

Edwin Emery.

I have often been asked to narrate my experience in the War of the Rebellion, and have as often refused, but now after the lapse of thirty three years since the close of that fearful struggle between brother men, I feel that perhaps it would be well, for the satisfaction of those who so earnestly desire it, to "Fight my battles over again."

Mine was not an exceptional experience, only that of many a boy of '61, but it may partly answer the question so often asked: "What did the privates do?"

I have often wondered how it happened that I, born of quaker stock on my mother's side (she was descended from the Kemptons, who were among the first settlers of our quaker city of New Bedford,) should have had such a natural leaning towards scenes of adventure and conflict. It may well have been that I inherited it from the paternal side of the house, for my father's father, John James, was taken prisoner on board his ship during the War of 1812, and thrown into an English prison, and I have often, during my childhood, listened to his tales of warfare and bloodshed, and longed to be a man that I might fight and avenge the wrongs inflicted on my devoted country in its earlier days; and how I wished, as I read of the War of the Revolution, that I might have lived in those stirring days, and done my part in creating the American Nation.

Certainly it did not seem possible that occasion would ever arise when I should be one of the defenders of that great nation.

The attack on Fort Sumter, the shot that so stirred the loyal hearts of the men of the North, awakened in me an ardent desire to enlist and help avenge the insult to our country's flag, but my father was so opposed to the idea that I reluctantly yielded to his authority until a few months later, during a visit to my brother in Woburn, Mass., I enlisted November 2nd 1861, just past my twentieth birthday, in Co. B, 1st Battalion, afterwards the 32nd Mass. Infantry. The company was raised by George L. Prescott, of Concord, Mass.

We were mustered into the United States service on November 27th, and on December 3rd were sent to Fort Warren, Boston harbor, to guard prisoners of war, among them being the confederate generals Buckner and Tilghman, Commodore Barron, Colonel Pegram, the confederate commissioners Mason and Slidell, the mayor and chief of police of Baltimore, and many others.

I remember an incident that may be of interest to which I was an eye-witness: , General Buckner was walking on the parapet, under guard, when a foreign man of war was being saluted in accordance with military usage; a large 32 lb. gun was belching forth half minute salutes; as he drew near it, wrapped in deep thought, not seeming to notice what was taking

place the order came to fire just as he was abreast
of the gun; he realized his danger and jumped forward just in time, for the next instant the gun was
discharged, and the prisoner must have felt that
it was indeed a narrow escape.

Many other interesting incidents connected with these celebrated prisoners occur to me,
but they would make my story too long.

We were drilled in the art of war during
all that winter, and under the strictest military
discipline, the commander of the fort being that
brave old martinet of the regular army, Colonel
Justin E. Dimmock. My brother George also
enlisted in the same company as myself and was
with me at Fort Warren, but the hardships and
exposures of that long cold winter and an attack
of typhoid fever undermined his health to such
an extent that he was discharged a short time
before we left Fort Warren for the seat of war
in the following May.

The hard and laborious life of the army
seemed to agree with me, and from the day of my
enlistment until the time I was wounded, more
than three years later, my health was perfect,
which was something to be thankful for, in the
army.

I did not regret leaving my brother behind me for I felt that one son was enough for my father to spare for his country's service; besides my brother had a wife and child, while I was young, with no mother to mourn for me, should I fall, and I felt that I could be spared better than those who had home ties, and that I could face hardships and dangers better than those who had families depending upon them. In short it seemed my duty and pleasure to go to the war.

CHAPTER II

TO THE SEAT OF WAR.

They turned from home, from wife and child,
  And all that life held sweet,
Into the hell of battle, calm
  They walked with steady feet,
Resolved for wounds and pain and death;
  In sacrifice complete.

Unknown.

On the 25th of May we left Fort Warren for the seat of war. Arriving at Washington we went into camp Alexander. June 30th our battalion, now composed of six companies, was ordered to join the army on the peninsula. Embarking on the transport Hero we arrived at Fortress Munroe July 2nd.

We continued on up the James river, landing at what was formerly President Harrison's plantation, on July 4th 1862. Now Legan

our soldier life in earnest, for fighting was then
going on; mud was knee deep and all was confu-
sion.   We were assigned to the brigade of Gen.
Charles Griffin, division of Gen. Morell, in Fitz
John Porter's command, afterwards the Fifth
Army Corps.

We were drawn up in line and given 80
rounds of ammunition.   Just then an officer rode
up covered with mud, and said: "Well boys, I
will give you a chance at the rebs; keep cool and
fire low!"   Off he went, and I was informed it
was Gen. George B. Mc Clellan.

We moved through a piece of woods, and
were opened upon by a battery.   It was getting to
be pretty warm, when the order came "Forward to
charge the battery," but before we could move, the
order was countermanded, and we retreated; this
was the end of the Seven Days Fight.

We camped upon the banks of the river
and staid there six weeks, every day sickness and
death reducing our ranks, for it was a very unhealthy place.   In fact it was the worst place
that could be imagined for a camp, marshy, wet
ground, dust and mud alternating; what wonder
is it that our men sickened and died?   Here on
August 9th Lieut. Nathaniel French Jr., one of

the most promising officers in our regiment died
of malarial fever.

Through it all my health remained perfect, and I was always ready for duty. Many
of our regiment were here detailed to act as
guards over the quartermaster's stores on the river bank.

Soon after our arrival at Harrison's Landing, President Lincoln visited and reviewed our
army. Our division stood in line from four
o'clock in the afternoon until after nine in the
evening, and then a party rode by in the moon-
light, one of whom was said to be the President
of the United States; as he was the only one who
wore a stove-pipe hat, we concluded that it must
be a fact, that we had been duly reviewed, and
gladly broke ranks and prepared our suppers.

On the night of August 1st the enemy
ran six pieces of artillery down on the opposite
side of the James river, and about midnight
opened upon our camp, and cold iron rained upon
us, ending our slumbers for that night. We had
two tents for the officers, and five for the men,
and solid shot went through them all, but we escaped serious injury, which seemed rather re-
markable. We were more than eager to leave

this sickly camp and life of inaction, but here we
had to stay and wait for marching orders.

CHAPTER III.

ON THE MARCH.

And we marched away to join the fray,
　Where the work of death was done,
And soon we stood where the battle clouds
　Hid the face of the mid-day sun.

'Mid the battle's din our ranks grew thin,
　And we dug our comrades' graves,
By brook and rill, by vale and hill,
　And laid away our braves.
                    Benj. Russell Jr.

Marching orders came on August 10th, and we gladly took up our line of march, passing through Williamsburg, Yorktown and Big Bethel to Newport News, where we boarded steamer Belvidere for Acquia Creek, thence by rail to Stafford Courthouse, near Fredericksburg. We were still kept on the move, and on August 27th we marched out on the Gainesville road, and

March 6, 1865.

formed in line of battle; here we had quite a
sharp brush with the enemy.   We were endeav-
oring to head him off in his march northward,
but were too late, and had to chase him as rapidly as possible.

I shall never forget the long and weary
march of the next day, which happened to be my
twenty-first birthday.   All that hot, dusty day
was spent in a forced march, and we suffered
greatly for water, of which there was none to be
had in that dreary country.   Along in the afternoon I came to a puddle of water covered with
green slime, in which partly lay a dead mule, who
had probably died while trying to slake his
thirst.   I did not take warning by him, but
brushed aside the green scum and took a drink;
it was wet and that was all that could be said of
it.

I dragged myself along until within an
hour of sunset, and then I dropped by the roadside as hundreds had done before me.   Our surgeon came along, and kindly urged me to keep
on, saying we were to camp in a piece of woods
about a mile further on; but I was too far gone
to stir then.   I rested an hour or so, and then
limped into camp; too weary to get anything to

eat or drink, I took off my equipments and without even unrolling my blanket, dropped upon the ground, and with my knapsack for a pillow, slept all night the dreamless sleep of a tired soldier.

When the boys reached camp, their first thought was to find water; there was but one well in the vicinity, and that was found under guard reserved for the headquarters mess. The indignant rank and file drove off the guard and helped themselves to the water.

Some of the boys, not knowing of the well, went into the swamp and dipped up the stagnant water there. No wonder there was a large amount of sickness after that time. It did not make me sick, but I felt rather lame when I awoke in the morning.

Next day, August 29th, we arrived on the old battle ground of Bull Run, in time to take part in the second battle of Bull Run. Again we had to fall back, and again we took up the line of march.

The next day we moved at 3 o'clock A. M. and camped at 11 P. M., after a march of twenty eight miles. At Chantilla we met the enemy on September 1st, but after a short engagement again kept on, marching through Georgetown into the state of Maryland. It was hot weather, and many of the men fell exhausted by the way; but we must not pause, for the enemy was still pressing northward and we must get between him and our own loved homes.

When we reached the South Mountain battle ground, that fierce conflict was over and they were burying the dead. I saw the body of General Reno who was killed in that battle. We had won a victory, but the loss was very heavy, and we had lost the gallant Reno, a serious blow for our cause. The idol of his men, they greatly mourned his loss.

"There was one poor fellow spoke up clear,
How he suffered before he died!
I am dying boys, but I feel no fear,
For I've fought by Reno's side."

CHAPTER IV.

ANTIETAM.

One summer morning a daring band
Of rebels rode into Maryland.
Over the prosperous, peaceful farms,
Sending terror and strange alarms,
The clatter of hoofs, and the clang of arms.

Fresh from the South, where the hungry pine,
They ate like Pharaoh's starving kine;
They swept the land like devouring surge,
A.d left their path to its furthest verge,
Bare as the track of the locust scourge.

Unknown.

Harper's Ferry had fallen, and Lee was gathering his army on the west bank of Antietam Creek in Maryland. When we reached the east side of the creek, we caught up to the main army under General McClellan on the 16th of September, just at sunset. We found the rebels to be well posted behind the top of the ridge on the other side of the stream.

The two armies now stood face to face, for McClellan's army was camped on the east side of the hills on the west branch of the Antietam. Our division was soon among them, and busy getting our supper, while we could see the smoke from the campfires of the opposing forces, where they too were preparing their evening meal.

What a beautiful sight it was after nightfall! The thousands of glowing campfires upon both hillsides made a picture upon my memory that time will never efface. After our weary march it seemed good to be here in camp, even though I knew a battle was to be expected the next day. I remember how peaceful and quiet everything seemed, and the cheerfulness of the men around me, showed how they enjoyed the welcome rest, and how little they thought of the conflict before them.

The 17th of September dawned fair and pleasant, but what a storm of death took place that day! The battle began at dawn and lasted until dark. The loss of life was terrible; the loss to the Union army alone was more than fifteen thousand men. We held the field, but on that narrow strip of ground between the Potomac river and Antietam Creek lay many thousands of brave men, while their comrades were so worn out with their terrible exertions that they could hardly find strength to care for the wounded or bury the dead.

Our regiment being on the reserve, supporting a battery, our loss was not heavy. On the 18th our corps relieved the ninth (Burnside's) corps at the lower bridge. On the 19th we expected another battle, but the enemy had retreated during the night. We pursued them through Sharpsburg, capturing many prisoners and several pieces of artillery. We went into camp and excepting a two days raid to Leestown, remained quiet until October 30th, when we started for Harper's Ferry and crossed the river into Virginia once more.

CHAPTER V.

UNDER ARREST.

Although the years have long gone by,
    And I ought to wear a wig,
I often give a smile or sigh,
    To the memory of that pig!

And how we carried him that day,
    Upon that weary tramp,
And thought that we would have a feast,
    When once we got to camp.

But when at last we stopped to rest,
    And cooked that little beast,
We never even got a bite,
    The general had the feast!
                    L. M. James.

My company was detailed to guard the ammunition train on its way back into Virginia. Before starting on the march, we had general orders read to us, forbidding all foraging in Maryland. On the first day's march towards

Harper's Ferry, several of the boys, myself included, noticed a number of small pigs in a field near the road.

As we had been on very short rations for about a week, it seemed to us a good chance to have a feast when we went into camp, so over the fence after the pigs we went. As I raised my gun to fire at a pig, I saw General Griffin, (who commanded our brigade,) and his staff, passing along the road on the further side of the wagons.

I waited until I thought he was beyond the sound of my rifle and then fired. The bullet passed through the pig, struck a stone, glanced, and went down the road, passing within a foot of the general's head, for he had stopped for a few moments, instead of riding on as I had supposed.

After I had shot the pig, one of the boys ran up and was using the butt of his gun to finish him and stop his squealing, when suddenly we were surrounded by the staff of Gen. Griffin! I made a break for the road, but found it was of no use, for the general himself stood by the fence, so back I went and with the rest of the boys was placed under arrest. Orders were given to march us to camp without rest, and carry the pig along, which we took turns in doing. It was a long pull, and when I could march no longer, down I sat. The guard repeated the order. "I am going to rest," I said. "Don't let the general see you," said the guard.

I did not rest long, but traveled all day without anything to eat, for we had left our haversacks and overcoats in the teams, which were now a long distance ahead.

At night we went into camp, then had to dress the pig, and it was cooked for the supper of the general and his staff, and we poor fellows got nothing. We pitched the general's tent and were then turned over to the provost guard. About eight o'clock I went under guard to the general's tent to do something he wanted done. "Guard, to your quarters," said the general, "This man will not run away!" "No, general, I will not," said I, and I quickly performed the duty required of me and went back to the provost guard.

At ten o'clock we were all sent under guard to our regimental headquarters. Our colonel had just rolled himself up in his blanket for the night and did not care to be disturbed. "Do you know where your company is?" he demanded:

"Yes sir" we answered, without any regard for facts.

"Go to it," he ordered, and we gladly started, free men once more. There were one hundred thousand men in the camp, and to find one small company in the middle of the night was no easy task, but about daylight we found the teams and our haversacks, got something to eat, and started off on the march again. So ended the only time in my life that I was a prisoner, or under arrest.

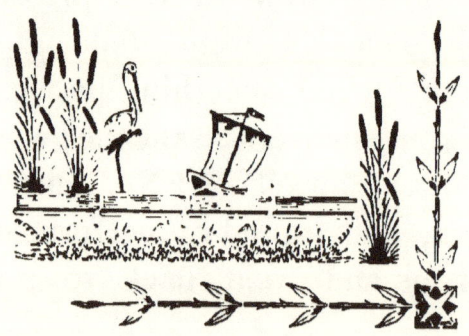

CHAPTER VI.

IN CAMP.

Comrades known in marches many,
Comrades tried in dangers many,
Comrades bound by memories many,
    Brothers ever let us be!

Wounds or sickness may divide us,
Marching orders may divide us,
But whatever fate betide us,
    Brothers ever let us be!
                    An old army song.

The Army of the Potomac, on November 10th, 1862, was massed near Warrington Virginia, where General McClellan was relieved from command of the army. I shall never forget the grief that was manifested by the soldiers on the removal of this popular commander. Ever mindful of the welfare and comfort of his men, he had won a warm place in their hearts, and enjoyed the respect and esteem that was never accorded any other commander.

The following verses were sung in camp and on the march long after he left us:

The order came, the die was cast,
McClellan was removed at last,
While far and near o'er hill and dale,
In thrilling notes the accents fell—
    "Come back to us McClellan!"

The bold, the brave, the fearless men,
When he had passed beyond their ken,
Bowed down their heads their tears to hide,
While still within their hearts they cried—
    "Come back to us McClellan!"

His chieftains came to say farewell,
And in the evening camp light fell,
The tears they strove in vain to hide,
While from their sorrow'd hearts they cried—
    "Come back to us McClellan!"

Go to the warriors on the field,
Charging upon the rebel steel,
And while they deal the fatal blow,
Hark to the cry, now high, now low—
    "Come back to us McClellan!"

Go to the soldier sorely tried,
Go to the sick one's lone bedside,
Stand by his cot, ere the soldier dies,
And listen to his feeble cries—
    "Come back to us McClellan!"

Go to the tented camping ground,
Where dirt and dust and mud abound,
And from the restless, slumbering ones,
In murmuring words the entreaty comes—
    "Come back to us McClellan!"

        Jonas A. Bigelow, U. S. A.

He was succeeded by General Burnside, and after a week of rest, we started for Falmouth Virginia, and on the 22nd went into camp at Stoneman's Switch. Here we remained most of the time all winter, although we expected every day to be ordered off on the march again for the unknown "Somewhere."

I well remember the hungry Thanksgiving day spent here. We were a long ways from our base of supplies at Acquia Creek, and all that we received was brought in wagons for several miles over hard and rough roads from Belle Plain.

For a week we lived on hard-tack, and the morning of Thanksgiving day, we received the last of the supplies in our regiment, half a cracker for each man. This was all we had until afternoon; our officers were out all the morning hunting in every direction for food, and at last succeeded in borrowing twenty boxes of hard-bread, which was all that the officers and men had that day.

How we thought of home that day and the good dinners that we had enjoyed on former festival days! How little our friends at home would have enjoyed their feast, could they have known that we were starving! In the course of the day I happened to see, near the tent where the officers bought their supplies, (for they did not draw rations like the rank and file,) a few beans that had been trodden down into the mud. I carefully picked them out, and perhaps got half a pint altogether, which I washed and stewed, and with my tentmate, made out our Thanksgiving dinner.

This was not the only time I have gone hungry; many a time have I suffered from hunger from cold, and from heat, but I shall ever remember that particular time, for it seemed to make me still more hungry as I thought of former Thanksgiving feasts, and the food I had wasted. But such are the fortunes of war, and we bore it as we did all other discomforts, as part of the price that must be paid, that our flag might again wave over an undivided country.

Chapter VII.

FREDERICKSBURG.

Of all the terrible sights of war,
The worst and most fearful sight,
Is the stubborn struggle of gallant men
In brave but unequal fight!
The useless charge and the shattered ranks,
And the slaughter and the flight!

Edward Willett.

Here we remained for some weeks, building ourselves log shanties, chopping wood, standing guard, being drilled, inspected, reviewed, and now and then going over towards the river and watching the confederates making their works good and strong, against the time when we were ready to attack them. While we were making ready, they were building and strengthening works, that would be beyond the power of mortal man to carry by assault, and yet that was what we were called upon to do, when at last General Burnside had got his army ready for active service. He had entirely re-organized the Army of the Potomac, which now numbered one hundred and twenty thousand men, divided into three grand divisions, each division consisting of two corps. Everything possible was done to strengthen our forces, and put us in good condition for active service; all this was not completed until the 11th of September.

The town of Fredericksburg is on the south side of the Rappahannock river, nearly opposite Falmouth. Back of the town is the range of hills called Marye's Heights, where Lee's army was strongly entrenched, when Gen. Burnside had got ready for business.

General Lee, with his three hundred cannon, covered the town and river, and his position was one of the strongest, yet Burnside persisted in his plan of attack, for on the morning of the 11th of December, at daybreak, the bugle sounded "Forward!"

It was a still, cold morning, and we started off in heavy marching order, our regiment leading, as it was our turn that day. We were in good spirits, although we knew that we had started out on a desperate attempt, and were en-route for Fredericksburg, three miles away. We marched to a point near the river and remained until the next day, when we crossed the river on pontoon bridges under a heavy fire from the enemy, with terrible loss of life.

On the 13th the bloody battle of Fredericksburg was begun, one of the most disastrous of the war. It was a useless, ill-judged endeavor to rout Lee's army from his impregnable position. In this battle more than thirteen thousand men were lost to the Union army, while the confederates lost less than half that number. My regiment lost thirty five men, killed and wounded. Defeated and disheartened, on the morning of the 16th, our army re-crossed the river and returned to our old camp.

On the 21st of January, 1863, we started on the "Mud march," about four o'clock in the morning. A bitter cold wind was blowing fiercely, and the air was full of sleet and rain. We marched all day and when we stopped for the night, made fires and sat around them all night to keep warm. The next day was warm as summer, but rainy; the mud grew deeper, as we struggled along, sinking in and being pulled out, taking us all day to go three miles. The whole country was under water, and you could not step without sinking above your shoes in mud. When we stopped for the night we could only lay down in the mud, or sit by the fires we managed, with much difficulty, to make.

The next day the water dried up a little, so we pulled down the fences and used the rails to corduroy the road. We returned to Stoneman's Switch, and re-constructed our shanties as well as we could, though we sadly missed the comforts we had destroyed before starting out, lest, in our absence, they might fall into the hands of the Johnnies.

We remained in camp until spring, and before that time arrived, Gen. Burnside was relieved, and General Hooker took his place. We gladly heard the order read that relieved him and appointed "Fighting Joe" as his successor.

Chapter VIII.

CHANCELLORSVILLE.

Ah I see you once more in your camp by the way;
Yes, again do I hear your guns in the fray!
In those tangled old woods you stood there in line,
While the foe was advancing! Ah boys, it was fine!
I remember it still, how they swept o'er the field
With their tiger like yell. They thought we would yield.
You stood like a rock, as all will agree—
My friends and my comrades of company B.

M. B. Duffie.

On April 27th 1863, we again started on our tour through Virginia. We crossed the Rappahannock at Kelley's Ford, marched to the Rapidan river, and went into camp on the south side. A brief rest, and again on the march, arriving at Chancellorsville, where we waged battle with the enemy from April 30th to May 5th. Here, on the 2nd of May, occurred the famous charge of the eighth Pennsylvania cavalry, numbering but three hundred men under Major Keenan, on Stonewall Jackson's leading division, keeping them back for a short time, giving our generals time to place their guns in position, thus saving our army from utter defeat. The tragic story is told by the poet Lathrop far better than I can tell it.

"Cavalry, charge!" not a man of them shrank,
Their sharp full cheer, from rank to rank,
Rose joyously with a willing breath,
Then forward they sprang, and spurred and clashed,
Shouted the officers, crimson sashed;
Rode well the men, each brave as his fellow,
In their faded coats of the blue and yellow:
And above in the air, with an instinct true,
Like a bird of war, their pennon flew.

With clank of scabbards and thunder of steeds,
And blades that shine like sunlit reeds,
And strong brown faces bravely pale,
For fear their proud attempt shall fail,
Three hundred Pennsylvanians close,
On twice ten thousand gallant foes!

Line after line the troopers came,
To the edge of the wood that was ringed with flame;
Rode in and sabred, and shot, and fell;
Nor one came back, of his wounds to tell.

Line after line, ay, whole platoons,
Struck dead in their saddles, of brave dragoons,

By the maddened horses were onward borne,
And into the vortex flung, trampled and torn;
As Keenan fought with his men, side by side,
So they rode, till there were no more to ride.

But over them lying there, shattered and mute,
What deep echo rolls? 'Tis a death salute,
From the cannon in place! For heroes, you braved
Your fate not in vain, the army was saved!

They have ceased. But their glory shall never cease,
Nor their light be quenched in the light of peace.
The rush of their charge is resounding still,
That saved the army at Chancellorsville!

George Parsons Lathrop.

We were defeated, and obliged to retreat, our brigade being detailed to cover the retreat of our army back over the river. We formed a line of battle, and as each division passed, we fell back a little nearer the river, still keeping our line of battle. Finally we were within half a mile of the river, where the last of our army were rapidly crossing on pontoon bridges. General Griffin, our brigade commander, had crossed the river on some duty assigned him, when he was informed that a large force of the enemy was rapidly approaching, and his brigade would inevitably be taken prisoners.

"If they are, I will be taken with them!" exclaimed our brave commander, and spurring his horse, he rapidly crossed on the pontoons, and

soon reached us, and marched us quickly to the
river, just as the confederates approached, intent
on gobbling us up.   We cut the fastenings of
the pontoons, and the bridge swung off down the
stream just in time, and we were all safely land-
ed on the other shore, happy to know that we
had escaped the horrors of a rebel prison, or death
at the hands of the merciless foe.

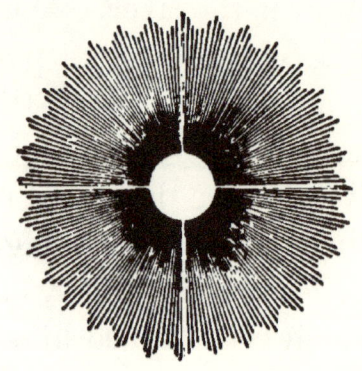

CHAPTER IX.

BRANDY STATION AND ALDIE.

Oh, tell me not their lives are lost,
Who to the death-shots yield,
But rather, write beneath their names,
"Promoted on the field!"

Unknown.

After the battle of Chancellorsville, the the thirty-second Massachusetts was detailed for guard duty on the railroad to Acquia Creek. We remained here but a short time however, for northward moved the enemy, and we on after them; at Brandy station on the 9th of June, we caught up with them, and had a sharp engagement, but failed to stop the march into Pennsyl-

vania.   Crossing the river towards Culpepper
Courthouse, past Morrisville, on to Manassas,
camping on the old battle ground on the night of
the 16th.

We had a tough march the next day, trav-
elling more than twenty miles; no water was to
be had, and we suffered greatly with the heat
and dust.   Our regiment started in the morning
with two hundred and thirty men, and camped
that night with one hundred and seven, of which
number I was one, and this was doing better than
any other regiment in our division.   Hundreds
of men dropped by the roadside, fainting and
dying from exhaustion; four died of sunstroke.
We heard indications of battle all day from the
direction of Aldie, and I suppose this forced
march was thought necessary, but I can truly say
that I much preferred all the horrors of the battlefield to these terrible long marches, when it
seemed impossible to keep up.   To drop out was
to lose sight of your regiment, and perhaps die
uncared for, or be gobbled up by guerrillas, who
were plentiful all through that God forsaken
country.

To be captured by guerrillas was sure
death or imprisonment, which to me seemed

worse than death on the field. It was during
this march that I acquired the nickname of
"Mosby," after the noted guerilla Colonel Mosby,
who was then making his dashing raids through
that region, causing his very name to be a terror
to all the inhabitants thereof.

I had picked up from the road where it
had been dropped, among other impedimenta by
the rebels we were pursuing, a gray cardigan
jacket, which, being much better than the one I
had worn so long, I had put on, and thrown a-
way the old one. I wore it into the battle of
Gettysburg a few days later, and had several
narrow escapes from being shot for a rebel by
our own men, on account of its color. As it was
all I had, I had to wear it, for we could draw no
clothing on the march.

Some little time after the Gettysburg
fight, I was on guard at the colonel's tent, and
he noticed my gray jacket, and enquired why I
wore it, and I told him it was all I had.

"I'll see that you have another, my boy," said
the colonel, and soon after, my captain provided
me with a new blouse, which I gladly donned,
discarding the gray one, which had but one fault
and that was its color. I could not discard the

nickname however, by which I am best remembered by some of my old comrades, who will never forget how I fought the Johnny rebs at Gettysburg, with a confederate's jacket on.

At Aldie occurred the great cavalry fight under Generals Pleasanton, Gregg and Kilpatrick. What a splendid sight it was! An event even in our eventful life to see those brave men move in battle line, with sabres drawn, steady as though on dress parade! Through the enemy's line they went, dealing death right and left. Not all of them came back, but those who did, came with victory perched upon their banners.

Then on we went, across the state of Maryland, encamping at midnight July 1st at Hanover, Pennsylvania, after a forced march of sixteen hours. By this time we were about worn out with so much marching and fighting, but there was no rest for us yet; for we had hardly dropped down for the night, when an aid arrived with orders to march directly to the aid of the First corps, which was fighting the whole rebel army at Gettysburg. So again we took up our weary line of march, pressing forward as fast as possible to the aid of our comrades. As we drew near Gettysburg, word passed down the line that General McClellan was again in command of the army.

How we shouted! How we cheered, and we moved on with quickened step, believing that our beloved general would lead us on to battle, and to victory! It was a false report, perhaps sent down the line to cheer our hearts and quicken our lagging feet. It served the purpose, but it was a sad disappointment, when we learned the truth.

Chapter X.

GETTYSBURG.

God send us peace! And where for aye the loved and lost recline,
Let fall, O South, your leaves of palm, O North, your sprigs of pine!
But when with every ripened year, we keep the harvest home,
And to the dear Thanksgiving feast our sons and daughters come,
When children's children throng the board in the old homestead
spread,
And the bent soldier of these wars is seated at the head,
Long, long the lads shall listen to hear the graybeard tell,
Of those who fought at Gettysburg, and stood their ground so well:
"'Twas for the Union and the flag!" the veteran shall say,
"Our grand old army held the ridge, and won that glorious day!"

Edmund Clarence Stedman.

We arrived on the field of Gettysburg at
nine o'clock A. M., July 2nd, and without rest
were ordered into the front line of battle. Our

brigade consisted of the 9th and 32nd Massachusetts, 4th Michigan, and 62nd Pennsylvania. We
had hardly got into line, when the enemy advanced directly upon us, and for an hour we had
it hot and heavy.

Here our regimental loss was heavy, but
we finally repulsed them, and soon after changed
position to a piece of woods bordering on the
wheatfield. Here a line was engaged in the
wheatfield, and the ground was covered with the
wounded and dead. We advanced and relieved
them, when the enemy charged us with such
overwhelming fury that we were obliged to fall
back.

Here Colonel Jeffers of the 4th Michigan
and a color sergeant of the same regiment were
killed, trying to save their flag, but it was captured, and a part of the regiment were taken
prisoners.

We could not stand the terrible storm of
leaden hail, and were retreating when our brigade
commander halted us and ordered us to face the
charging enemy. It was a fatal act for many
of the Thirty-second! We fought our way back
inch by inch, union and confederate men inextri-
cably mingled; so we fought until we gained the

shelter of the woods. I had lost my regiment,
but saw the Pennsylvania Bucktails fixing bayonets for another charge, so I stepped into their
ranks to charge with them, when I saw my regimental colors, with four of the color guard near
by, so joined them and waited for the boys to
rally under the old flag, when we again advanced
into the bloody fray.

I look back with pride upon the valor
shown that day by my brave comrades; at Little
Roundtop, the Wheatfield, in the Loop, many a
brave boy of the 32nd gave up his life, in that
terrible struggle. Our regiment carried into the
fight 227 men, and we lost 81 killed and wounded. My tentmate, Dwight D. Graves, went
down severely wounded in the foot, and another
comrade, Calvin P. Lawrence, was left on the
field with a broken leg when we fell back. As
the rebs charged over him, one of them turned to
bayonet him, but his lieutenant prevented him,
and asked the wounded man,

"Where's your men now?"

"You just keep on, you'll find them!" was the
reply, as the men swept over him. Soon they
rushed back in full retreat, and our brave comrade shouted after them, "I say, leftenant, I

guess you found them." We kept the field, and
all that night I spent looking over the battle
ground for wounded comrades, giving to one a
drink of water from my canteen, placing a knapsack under the head of another, covering another
from the chilly air with a blanket picked up on
the field, and doing what I could to relieve their
suffering.

Morning came, and our brigade remained
near Little Round Top, receiving our full share
of the storm of iron hail, throughout the artillery
duel of the third day. Then came Pickett's desperate charge, the final effort of the enemy, who
never got further north than here. Then came
the retreat of the enemy, and our pursuit of them
back into Virginia.

During the battle, my cousin, James A.
Shepard, of the 18th Massachusetts received his
death wound, while going to a spring to fill several canteens for his comrades. I saw him the
day before the battle bright and cheerful. I
heard he was wounded, but did not learn of his
death until some days after, when a letter from
home gave me the following account of his death
and burial.

He was shot in the shoulder, severing an

artery, and died in a Philadelphia hospital a few days after the battle, but lived to see his widowed mother, who was telegraphed for, at his request.

When she arrived at the hospital, she stood a moment at the door of the ward where her boy lay on his deathbed, and where the long rows of beds and their occupants all looked alike to her; she heard his voice at the further end of the room, saying "Oh mother, mother! here I am come quick!" and soon the heartbroken mother knelt by his bedside, while he, happy in her presence, talked of the battle and tried to comfort her.

"I know I've got to die," he said, "But never mind, mother dear, it is in a glorious cause, and we whipped the rebels good!" Poor boy, he was only twenty, yet was willing to die for his country!

As he grew weaker, he talked of the dear ones at home, and wished he could have bade them goodbye.

"Kiss them for me, mother," he said, "And take me home, and lay me beside my father, and put some flowers on my grave from the dear old home garden, that I have so longed to see!"

His mother remained with him until he died, and through untold difficulties, she brought his body home, being obliged to smuggle it part of the way, and now, in the family lot, he lies beside his father and mother. Two of his brothers also lie buried there, Charles, who served in the Massachusetts heavy artillery, and George, who was badly wounded in the head while serving in the navy; he never fully recovered, and died soon after the war ended.

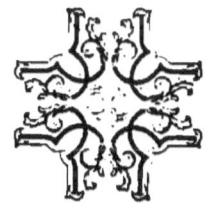

CHAPTER XI.

MINE RUN.

We wait for the bugle, the night winds are cold,
The limbs of the soldiers feel jaded and old.
The field of our bivouac is windy and bare,
There is lead in our joints, there is frost in our hair,
The future is veiled, and its fortune unknown,
As we lie with hushed breath till the bugle is blown.

Thomas B. Higginson.

We crossed the river near Berlin, keeping east of the Blue Ridge. At Manassas Gap on July 23rd, we saw some pretty fighting by the Third Corps, and on the 8th of August, we went into camp at Beverly Ford, and remained five weeks, enjoying our well earned rest. Here I saw five deserters shot Sept. 15th we moved to Culpepper, where I saw a bounty jumper drummed out of camp, branded with the letter D. Here

we received 180 recruits, and between October
10th and 29th, we were marching back and forth,
to one point and then another, as though our
generals thought we needed exercise.

November 29th, 1863 found us in line of
battle at Mine Run. For three days and nights
we faced the enemy, and awaited the signal to
open the battle. I shall never forget one night,
the coldest I ever saw in Virginia. Mine Run
was a little stream of water made formidable by
the rebels, whose works were back of it. The
stream was filled with thorny bushes and brush,
now frozen in; when across that, there was a
strong abattis made of sharpened timber, that
must be removed before we could charge the enemy, strongly entrenched behind earthworks.
Not much charging could be done in that situation, and we old soldiers knew the hopelessness
of such an attempt.

We knew that the order had been given
to charge on the enemy's works at daybreak.
We felt rather gloomy, for we knew that death
was certain, if we made that desperate attempt.
For my part, I had faced many dangers, had been
under fire many times, but had never felt, as I
did then, that death stared me in the face. The

horrors of that bitter cold night can never be told. All night long we had to keep in motion to avoid freezing to death, for no fire could we have, lest we be discovered by the enemy; more than one poor fellow was frozen to death in the rifle pits.

Morning came at last, but we heard no order to charge. All honor to General Meade, who has been censured for his failure to charge across Mine Run. With all his bravery, he was too humane to order such a useless sacrifice of life, though he knew he incurred censure and probably disgrace, in ordering a retreat instead. Silently we retreated out of our dangerous situation, and made our way towards Stephensburg. Hungry and cold as we were, we hurried along, halting now and then just long enough to build a little fire and boil some coffee, the soldier's best friend.

Towards night it grew warmer, and when the order came to halt for the night on an open plain, we were too tired to do anything but drop in our tracks, rolled up in our rubber blankets. When we awoke in the morning, we found that several inches of snow had fallen during the night, and covered that vast body of sleeping men as with a white and fleecy blanket. We soon had fires and a warm breakfast. By ten o'clock the snow had melted, and we took up our march with renewed courage.

Our army crossed to the north side of the Rappahannock river, and two days after found us encamped at Liberty, near Bealton Station, on the Orange and Alexandria railroad, and here we had a brief respite from our toils and dangers.

CHAPTER XII.

A LETTER FROM THE FRONT.

"Halt! Who goes there?" My challenge cry,
　It rings along the watchful line,
"Relief!" I hear a voice reply;
　"Advance and give the countersign!"
Unknown.

Camp at Liberty Va., Dec.— 1863.

You ask me about our daily life, and now, while "All is quiet upon the Potomac," I will try to give you some idea of company B's life in camp.　Reveille is sounded at sunrise; our company falls into line, and the first sergeant calls the roll.

Each man then cooks his own breakfast, except when two or three tentmates agree to take

turns.   In my case, my tentmate does the cook-
ing, and I get the wood and water.   Our rations
when in camp are generally hardtack, pork, salt,
sugar, coffee, beans, potatoes, fresh meat, etc.,
but we do not draw all of these things at once;
some days we will draw hardtack and pork, sugar and coffee; on other days, fresh meat, and potatoes.

In drawing rations for the regiment, the
quartermaster draws up a requisition for as many
rations as there are men in the regiment; they
are sent to regimental headquarters, and divided
among the companies.   The first sergeant of
each company receives it, and divides it among
the men.

One day's rations consists of ten hardtack,
half a pound of salt pork, a few spoonfuls of
coffee, and the same of sugar.   In drawing
fresh meat, it is cut up into pieces, the orderly
calls the roll, beginning one day at A, and the
next at Z, and as each man's name is called, he
steps up, takes his choice of the meat, and the
last is "Hobson's choice."

After breakfast, surgeon's call is sounded,
and if sick or unfit for duty, the boys report to
him; he gives them pills or quinine, and reports

them either fit for duty, or sick in quarters.
His word is law, and if he understands his calling, he seldom makes mistakes; but I have known
many instances where men have been reported
for duty, who were not fit to be out of their
bed.

Next, the orderly makes the detail for
camp guard, police, picket, etc.   At 8 o'clock
A. M., camp guard is placed on duty around the
camp, and remains so for twenty-four hours, two
hours on post, and four off.   Those detailed for
police duty, are placed under a non-commission-
ed officer, and set to cleaning up camp.

The pickets fall in, and after all the de-
tails from the various companies get together,
they are marched to the front, and are posted so
that the whole front is guarded, relieving those
that have been on duty.   They remain on duty
for twenty-four hours, two hours on post, and
four off, except when very near the enemy, in an
exposed position, then they sometimes remain for
several days.

After the pickets go on duty, we who are
not detailed for duty, have about two hours to
ourselves, in which to wash and mend our clothes,
clean our rifles and equipments, etc.   At 10.30

o'clock we go on company drill, which lasts an hour, after which, we get our dinner.

After dinner we have battalion drill, brigade drill, or something else to keep us busy, and out of mischief.

Dress parade comes at sunset, tattoo at 9 o'clock, taps at 9.30; all lights must then be out, and the army is at rest.

Chapter XIII.

RE-ENLISTED.

Two years have passed; those gallant men
Have kept the oath that they made then.
On many a field their valor's shone,
On many a field their bones are strewn;
They've bravely fought and still shall fight.
For Union, and the cause of right!
Till rebel hosts shall yield the way,
To Union arms, and Union sway.

J. B. C.

The die is cast! Come life or death,
My Country! I will faithful be,
Until o'er all thy wide domain,
Shall wave the banner of the free.

L. M. J.

It was at Liberty that most of the members of the 32nd Massachusetts re-enlisted for three years more. I was not the first to re-enlist; I knew now what a soldier's life really was. I realized that my father knew what he was talking about, when he told me that it was no holiday picnic, and that the men of the South were as brave as those of the North, and that it would take years instead of months to conquer them, as so many thought when the war began. I had endured two years of hardships and dangers, and longed for a peaceful life with those I loved at home. I knew my dear old father would be grieved, were I to again enlist.

I fought it all out alone on picket, that cold long night, went back to camp, and with fingers almost too stiff with cold to hold the pen, signed my name to the paper that bound me to the service of my country for "Three years more, or until the close of the war."

Yes, I had made up my mind, that come what would, I would see it out! My country needed me; dire disaster had overtaken it, dark and gloomy was the situation, and now more than ever, were needed strong and willing hands to defend it; and so I would do my duty, and leave the rest to God.

And now, looking back over the long years since that day, I can truly say, I have never regretted my decision. The terrible year that followed would have been included in my first term of enlistment of three years, and so I did not serve quite a year longer than I would have done, if I had not re-enlisted. Many a poor fellow who felt that three years was enough, and that he could not endure such a life any longer than that, and consequently did not re-enlist, lost his life in the battle summer that followed. But none could foresee the future, and the close of the war looked to us in the field, as a long way ahead.

So many of the regiment re-enlisted that we were given 30 days furlough, and allowed to go home as a regiment. We had previously had re-enforcements from time to time, so that there were 3 40 who re-enlisted, and started for home, arriving in Fall River by the New York boat, on January 17th, 1864.

CHAPTER XIV.

AT HOME AGAIN.

From every height our banners bright, their flashing folds display!
The trumpet's tongue is jubilant with stirring notes today.
The cannon and the merry bells join with our vast array,
    And sound a welcome home!

Ye have come from the battlefields of glory and of blood,
Where like a rock ye firmly met rebellion's rushing flood,
Where o'er the traitors' reeling ranks triumphantly ye stood,
    To find a welcome home.
        James B. Congdon.

As the day of our arrival was the Sabbath, which we dimly remembered was kept sacred at the North, the commanding officer telegraphed to Governor Andrew to know if it would do to take his men through Boston on the Sabbath day. He quickly received the answer, "Come right along!" So he issued orders to the men to be as orderly as possible, and not shock the pious people of the Puritan state, and we took the train to Boston.

How astonished the war worn soldiers were at their reception! Ours was the first Massachusetts regiment returning with the proud title of "Veteran," and the people had turned out *en masse* to do us honor. We marched through crowded streets to the State House, where we received a welcome from the Governor, and a salute was fired in our honor, on the Common; then to Faneuil Hall, where a most sumptuous dinner was prepared for us, of which we were invited to partake, by the Mayor of Boston.

After dinner, Governor Andrew made an address that will, I think, ever be remembered by the members of the old 32nd. I cannot remember all he said, but some of his eloquent words still linger in my memory:

I cannot, soldiers of the Union Army, by words, in a fitting measure, repeat your praise. This battle-flag, riddled with shot and torn with shell, is more eloquent than human voice, more pathetic than song. This flag tells what you have done, it reveals what you have borne, and it shall be preserved as long as a thread remains, a memorial of your valor and patriotism.

I give you praise from a grateful heart, in behalf of a grateful people, for all you have suffered, and all you have accomplished; and while I welcome you to your homes, where the war-worn soldier may rest a brief while, I do not forget your comrades

in arms who have fallen, fighting for that flag, defending the rights
and honor of our common country. The humblest soldiers who have
given their lives away, will be remembered as long as our country
shall preserve its history.

As the people gazed on the torn and
blackened remnant of the beautiful silk flag we
had borne away with us two years before, it
seemed to tell more eloquently than words could
do, of battles won and lost. And now, after the
lapse of thirty-four years, it still, with other battle flags, is preserved in a glass case in the State
House at Boston. If you should look for it
there, it might be difficult to find it among the
many handsome banners hanging there, for it
is a mere strip of silk that seems to be just
hanging by a few threads to the staff, a black
and ragged remnant of the beautiful silk flag we
took with us to the front; but we old soldiers are
far more proud of it than we were in the days
when it was first presented to us, before it had
been consecrated by the blood of the brave boys
who bore it through the storm of battle, and gave
their lives, rather than the flag should be lost to
the regiment. We had a new flag to take back
with us, and that also bears the marks of shot and
shell, and is sacredly preserved.

After the dinner was over, we were dis-

missed, and I made quick time to New Bedford,
where I received a warm welcome from my father, who was overjoyed to see me.

The first night at home, I went to bed in
my old room, but could not sleep, the feather
bed was too soft for me; at last I got up, rolled
myself in a blanket, and laid down on the floor,
where I slept like a top. The feather bed was
removed next day, and I slept very comfortably
after that on the straw mattress.

How the happy days flew by, when friends
vied with each other in making my furlough
pleasant for me, and doing their best to spoil my
appetite for army rations, with their cakes, pies,
and all sorts of good things!

But all too soon we had to say goodbye.
On February 17th we once more started for the
South, arriving at camp Liberty two days later,
warmly welcomed by the comrades we had left
there, and proud of the title of "Veteran," with
all that it implied.

CHAPTER XV.

IN THE WILDERNESS.

In that valley down there, where the wild ivies creep,
The night birds stand sentry o'er comrades asleep,
Their graves are now sunken, the headboards decayed,
And the trenches are crumbled, where fought our brigade.
Through rifts in the forest, if your vision is keen,
The breastworks we builded, can dimly be seen.

M. B. Duffie.

General Grant now took command of the army, and on April 30th 1864, we broke camp at Liberty, and began the hardest, most bloody campaign of the war. Our division gathered near Rappahannock Station; crossed the river for the fifteenth time, and marched to Brandy Station, marching almost constantly. We crossed the Rapidan at Germania Ford, marched all the next day, camping at night in the Wilderness, very near the enemy. May 5th we threw up earthworks, but at noon advanced, leaving our works to other troops. We were soon heavily engaged, and so began Bloody May.

From this time forward, day and night, marching, fighting, digging earthworks, there was no rest for us. From losses in battle, and from sickness, our regiment again dwindled down to a company in numbers.

On May 8th we supported the 5th Massachusetts battery, with some pretty smart fighting. On the 9th we again went to the front, and threw up works, behind which we kept pretty close most of the day. Sharpshooters were plenty in the rebel lines, not far from us. One of my company, George Erskine, who was near me in the works, sat on a cracker box, and turned his head to speak to me, thereby exposing himself a little, and as I was looking at him, I saw a bullet strike the side of his head, go through it, and strike the ground. He gave one sigh, and fell dead at my feet. It was the work of a rebel sharpshooter.

A little later in the day, the orderly sergeant asked—

"Who will go out on the skirmish line?"

The skirmish line was about a third of a mile in

front of us, and to reach it, one had to run the gauntlet, for the enemy had a fair view of the whole field, and they improved it, you may be sure.

Several comrades volunteered, and went under a sharp fire. I felt a little ashamed of myself for not going too, so I said to my chum,

"If he calls for more, I am going!"

"I go if you do," said dear old Dwight, and soon the word came again,

"Who will volunteer?"

"I will go for one!" Said I, and Dwight said the same.

Over the works we went, the minie balls singing and zipping at us as we made our best time over that open field. We reached the line all right, and settled down to business.

After a time I found my ammunition was getting low, and by the time it was all gone, it was growing dark, so that we could move round with less danger, for we could not show ourselves without drawing the fire of the sharpshooters, so at dark I went round among the dead, and took all the ammunition I could find, and began again where I left off. We remained within two hundred yards of the enemy's works all night. During the night, our officers sent us plenty of ammunition, and informed us that we were to charge at noon next day, and that we were to fall into line as they advanced, but for some reason, the expected charge was delayed.

Chapter XVI.

LAUREL HILL.

Through a vista bright of the years long fled,
By the flag-decked graves of our comrades dead,
By the tints of summer, and the winter's white,
By the sheen of noon, and the shades of night,
There hangs a scene of the olden days,
With a warp of blue, and a woof of gray.
I will cut the web from out the loom,
And place it today 'mid the May-day bloom.

Three times amid the brake they form,
Three times upon the guns they storm,
Three times the army holds its breath,
To see those charges grand of death.

S. D. *Richardson.*

For two or three days we remained on the skirmish line, digging rifle pits to protect ourselves from the fire of the enemy. These were holes in the ground deep enough for one or more men to stand in, and if we showed our heads we were pretty sure to draw their attention, so we kept out of sight as much as possible. But our greatest peril was from our own line, a quarter of a mile in the rear of us, for there were several pieces of artillery continually sending shells and solid shot over our heads into the enemy's lines, and some of them were too near us for comfort and safety, for we were on slightly rising ground in front of them, and the gunners, to do more execution, depressed their pieces so much that every now and then a shot or shell would skim by, or over us, as we hugged the ground.

We would watch for the flash of the guns, and drop to the ground, so the shot generally went over us. In the rifle pit with me were two of my comrades, one of whom had taken off his haversack, and laid it near by. A shot from our line struck that haversack, and sent it flying in every direction.

Comrade Flint was fairly peppered with pieces of tin plate, cup, knife, fork and spoon, which wounded him severely in several places. He stood the pain as long as he could, and finally said he was going back to the lines; we advised him to wait until dark, but the pain was so great that he could not, and he started on the run across the open field, back to our main line. Instantly he was a target for the rebel sharpshooters. We watched him anxiously, and once saw him go down, but he was up and off in a moment, and reached our lines, where he went into the hospital.

He received a wound in the leg, from which he never fully recovered. The other wounds healed after a while, but left indelible scars.

Soon after, the firing ceased, and we felt better, when we were no longer in danger from our own artillery.

At last, on the morning of the 12th came the order to attack, and our gallant little brigade commanded by Colonel Prescott, dashed across the field as far as the foot of Laurel Hill. How our brave boys charged those works under that heavy shower of grape and canister, none who survived will ever forget!

But we could not take the works, and had to fall back, under a galling fire from their whole line. Oh! What a shower of death came down upon us! Before we got our colors back to our old position, the 32nd had lost five color bearers, and one hundred and three, out of one hundred and ninty men, killed or wounded. A number of the boys of our company lay killed or wounded upon the field we had charged over, and the constant firing along the whole line of the enemy's works, made it dangerous business going out to bring them in; but several of us determined to do so, in spite of the risk we incurred.

Before leaving home we had made a solemn promise to each other, that no man should be left unburied or uncared for on the field; that we would risk life and limbs that our wounded should be cared for, and our dead comrades tenderly laid in the bosom of mother earth. We usually waited until night before going out after our fallen comrades, but we could see the poor fellows lying there under the scorching sun, and felt that some of them would not hold out until night.

Taking a blanket for a stretcher, four of us started out on the run, drawing upon us a deadly fire from the enemy. One of our party fell, wounded in the leg, but the rest managed to take him along in our hasty retreat. Again and again we made the attempt, succeeding in getting most of our wounded under cover.

Night came, and we started out to bury our dead. Many a poor fellow lying upon his face, did I turn over in my search for my comrades that night. Suddenly I came upon one of my company, still living, but mortally wounded. He had been shot through the spine, and could not be moved, so I made him as comfortable as possible by putting a blanket under his head, and giving him some water. His sufferings were terrible, but soon over; he knew his time had come, and gave me messages for his folks and friends at home.

I promised him that I would write and let them know how, and when he died, and that I would see that he was buried. I remained with him until death released him from his agony, then closed his eyes, and covered him with his blanket.

Sadly I left him, and moved on to where I could hear a well known voice calling for help. It was another of my company badly wounded, but able to be moved, so I hastily rolled him into a blanket, and we soon had him within our line.

Busy all night, when daylight came, we had buried our dead, and gathered in our wounded, thus fulfilling the compact that was never broken when it was possible for us to keep it.

What a comfort it was to us, that solemn promise, for, far worse than death, was the thought
of lying exposed and unburied on the battlefield.
That night was a sad one, never to be forgotten
by me, when we rolled our comrades up in their
blankets, and laid them in graves that will forever remain unknown.

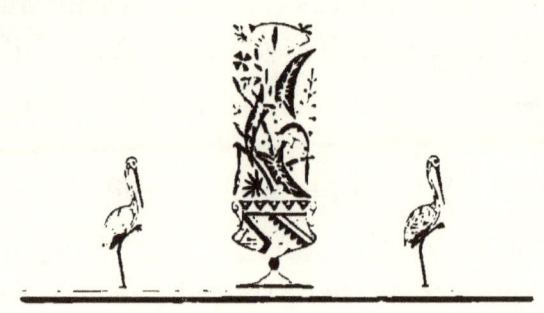

Chapter XVII.

THE WILDERNESS CAMPAIGN.

Yes, it all appears to my mind like a dream,
How we filed out of camp, and forded that stream.
Through the storm we have struggled, by day and by night;
For our flag and our country, we wrought with our might.
On that dangerous post, through the dews and the damp,
We have guarded from ill, our slumbering camp.

M. B. D.

From the 12th to the 23th, our regiment was constantly under fire from the enemy in front of us, at Spottslylvania Courthouse. and vicinity, continually changing our location, throwing up earthworks each night after a weary day's march, before we could roll ourselves in our blankets, and take our short night's rest.

On the morning of the 23rd, we took up our line of march towards the North Anna river, crossing it at Jericho Ford, our brigade advancing at once in line of battle into a piece of woods, where we had a skirmish with the enemy, who fell back, and we proceeded to fell trees, and build a line of works.

Before we had finished them, the enemy in force, under General Hill, attacked us, and endeavored to drive us out of our works and into the river. The assault fell mainly upon our division. Our regiment was on the left of the line of battle, and we did our best to give them a warm reception. For the first time since the campaign began, we fought in our works. It was a short, sharp fight, and the enemy was repulsed.

We remained in our works until morning, when we moved on towards Hanover Junction, but on May 26th we received orders to retire, which we did during the night, and once more crossed the North Anna river at Quarles Ford, and marched almost constantly for twenty-four hours towards the Pamunky river.

We next met the enemy near Mechanicsville, on the morning of the 30th of May. Little did we think then, that in the future years, that day would be set apart for honoring the memory of the fallen sons of the nation, our brigade advanced in line of battle through Tolopotomy Swamp, driving the confederate skirmishers until we came to open fields near Shady Grove Church, where we found the enemy in force behind earthworks.

We could not take them, so kept back as much as we could, out of range, yet our loss during the day was twenty-two, killed or wounded. I shall never forget our march through Tolopotomy woods, keeping in line, over briars and fallen trees and stumps. Our shoes were worn out with twenty five days of constant marching and fighting, and we were about as bad off ourselves. But we got there all the same, and staid there until midnight, when we were relieved by a part of the Ninth Corps, and went into camp, where we remained on the reserve for two or three days.

We took this time to do a little much needed washing, for we had no change of clothing, being in very light marching order. During our long marches, often, when we came to a stream, have I taken off my shirt, given it a hasty wash, wrung it out, put it on again, and gone on my way rejoicing.

Perhaps the simple record kept in my diary during that "Bloody May," as it has been so often called, will give some idea of the life we led when we were constantly confronting the enemy, with, as we might well say, a musket in one hand, and a shovel in the other; we could not stop to rest without first shoveling up earthworks to protect us from the fire of the ever active enemy.

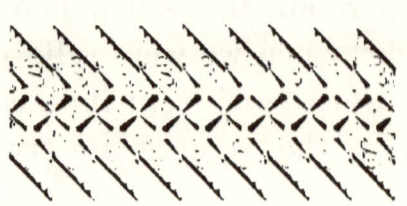

CHAPTER XVIII.

LEAVES FROM MY DIARY.

That starry banner blazed afar,
  The ensign of the free;
The beacon light of millions past,
  And millions yet to be.
Thy father loved its shining folds,
  He followed where they waved,
Thro' tangled wood, or frowning height,
  As battle's storm he braved.
                    Mrs. Ralston.

May 1 1864. Was relieved from picket last
night, broke camp, went within one mile of Rappahannock Station. To-day crossed the Rappahannock river, and marched to Brandy Station.
Corporal Tuttle left for home.

May 2. In camp near Brandy Station; sent

letters home.　Several of the boys left us, having exchanged into the navy.

May 3.　Broke camp at one o'clock P. M. Camped near Culpepper.

May 4.　Broke camp last night at eleven o'clock; marched through Stephensburg, crossed the Rapidan at Germania Ford at eight A. M.; camped at one P. M., after marching fourteen hours.

May 5.　In the Wilderness.　Left camp, advanced half a mile, and threw up breastworks; skirmishing began, and we advanced into the fight, which was very hot work.　Fell back to our works at night.

May 6.　Left our line at three A. M. and went to the front; heavy skirmishing from daylight till dark.　There has been some hard fighting on our left.　At dark we went to the rear, then back to the front, where we stayed until midnight, then returned to our works.

May 7.　Was awakened about sunrise by heavy firing all along the line.　Our brigade made a charge over the works; some fighting all day.

May 8.　Sunday.　We moved to the right at ten P. M. last night.　Came up with the enemy at eight this morning; heavy fighting. We are driving the enemy. Our regiment supported the Fifth Mass. battery. Our brigade charged the rebs works, with a loss of three hundred men. Fighting near Spottsylvania Courthouse.

May 9. Started at ten o'clock last night, and went to the front. This morning threw up some works, and laid in them all day. No fighting in front of us, only skirmishing until sunset, then we had some hard fighting. Volunteered, and went out skirmishing. Erskine, of my company killed to-day. We were attacked twice, but the enemy was repulsed.

May 10 Our regiment supported the First New York battery to-day. Fighting began at half past eleven, and lasted until night. John Tidd and E. B. Hewes of my company wounded. Received a week's mail; no letters for me.

May 11. Still supporting the First New York battery. Sent a letter home written on paper picked up on the battlefield.

May 12. Went out skirmishing at three o'-clock this morning. Flint of my company, badly wounded. Later charged the enemy's works. Wellington and Dowd of my company killed.

May 13. Was relieved from skirmish line,

and went to the regiment, then we started for somewhere: stopped in the woods. Lost my knapsack and every thing I had.

May 14. Up in front; staid here all day, but not much fighting. Within a mile of Spottsylvania.

May 15. In front; no fighting. Formed in line of battle in advance of our works, expecting to charge the enemy's works, but did not, for some reason to me unknown.

May 16. Laid in line of battle all day and night; no fighting. On guard.

May 17. Laid in line of battle until dark, and then advanced, and worked all night throwing up works.

May 18. Shelling began early this morning. Laid behind works all day and night. Received seven letters from home, the first I have had since we broke camp at Liberty, and they are very welcome.

May 19. Laid behind our works until about sunset, then fighting began on our right. Packed up and moved to the right. Commenced a letter to father.

May 20. Laid in line of battle behind our works. Sent letter to father.

May 21. Laid behind our works until one P. M. Packed up and moved to the left; camped at eight o'clock P. M. Received letters from home.

May 22. Broke camp at four this morning, but did not start until ten o'clock. Came up with some of the enemy about two P. M. Stopped for dinner at four o'clock, then went on picket.

May 23. We started this morning at six o'clock, and crossed the North Anna river near Hanover Junction. Skirmishing began as soon as we crossed, at three P. M.; fighting began about an hour before sunset. Smart fight.

May 24. Threw up some works and laid behind them until five P. M. Packed up and moved to the right, then front, and threw up some works.

May 25. Started this morning at half past four, and advanced about two miles, then skirmishing began. Threw up some works.

May 26. Laid behind earthworks until dark, then started, and marched until eleven P. M., when we stopped for rations. Atwood wounded to-day. Two years ago we left Fort Warren for the front.

May 27. Marched all night until half past six this morning, then stopped for breakfast near Reed's Church. Stopped there two hours, then marched until half past five P. M. Marched for twenty-two hours.

May 28. Started this morning at half past five. Crossed the Pamunky river, and went about a mile; stopped for breakfast, and then threw up some works. Received letters from home.

May 29. Advanced two miles, rested two or three hours, then advanced another mile, when skirmishing began. Threw up some works, and stopped all night.

May 30. Packed up and started at seven this morning; skirmishing began as soon as we started Advanced two miles, fighting all the way. Our regiment charged the enemy, with a loss of thirty men.

May 31. Regiment relieved, and sent to the rear for a brief rest. Received letters from the dear ones at home.

CHAPTER XIX

COLD HARBOR.

Ah me! I see it all again,
  The frenzied battle's formless form,
The reeling field, alive with men,
  The thunderous flashes through the storm!

The rifle's crack, the hiss, the thud;
  The sizz of the on-hurtling shell;
The dying cry; the trickling blood—
  The sights, the sounds we knew too well.
                    Rev. Minot J. Savage.

On the 3rd of June, before daylight, we were called up to do our part in the battle of Cold Harbor. The troops that had relieved us at the front the day before had been driven from their works, and our division was called upon to re-take them.

It was the same along the whole line. We were to charge across an open field, under a terrible fire from the enemy, strongly entrenched behind earthworks. Between our line of works and that of the enemy, the ground was covered with pine trees, felled and fastened across each other, and in addition, they had posted a battery in a position that could sweep the entire unsheltered field. We heard afterwards that Lee had been two weeks getting ready for us.

It was about half past four on that bright June morning, that we started on that memorable charge. Never shall I forget the storm of bullets, grape and canister that was rained upon us. My comrades fell on my right and left till I thought there would be none left to tell the tale. Half way across, my shoe became untied, and I knew that I would lose it unless I tied it up again, so down on one knee I went, and tied my shoe.

My comrades saw me drop, and I heard a shout, "Mosby's hit!" I was up in an instant, and on with the rest. On we went until we reached the works, from which we drove the enemy, but they only fell back to their own line of works, about two hundred yards away. We remained in the recaptured works, and kept up a constant exchange of fire all day long; on neither side could a man show his head without being shot at, but we hindered them as much as we could from using their battery upon us.

I remember one poor fellow of my company, who had somehow gone to a part of our line where the enemy had a raking fire right among us. I noticed him lying there as though asleep, but I well knew that no one living could sleep in that place, and concluded that he must be dead. I offered to help his brother bring him in, but he demurred, fearing that he might share the same fate. We did not know what moment we might have to leave, and did not want to leave a dead comrade unburied.

At last four of us started after the body, and succeeded, under a terrific shower of bullets that drove us back more than once, in getting him onto a blanket, and each one holding a corner, we made quick time into the rifle pits. We rolled the poor fellow in the blanket, and buried him in one of the rifle pits; many a poor fellow was buried in that way.

There was a peach orchard between the lines, and when the battle ended at dark, there was not much left of it but the trunks of the trees. All day I kept pegging away. When my gun got too foul from constant firing. I poured in a little water, washed it out, snapped a cap or two, and I was ready for action again. I was not sorry however, when nightfall put an end to the conflict, and I could drop down and rest.

Another charge was ordered before night, all along the line, but the order was countermanded, thus saving many precious lives. The loss of our army that day was over thirteen thousand men, our regimental loss being ten killed, and twenty-one wounded.

The next morning at daybreak I heard the orderly call my name, and reported to him immediately, and received the order with others,

"On the skirmish line!"

While I stood waiting a few moments for the skirmishers to get together, I noticed a Johnny Reb walking over to our line; I thought he wanted to come in, so I shouted to him to come on in; he stopped and looked at me a moment as though surprised, then turned on his heel, and walked back from whence he came, taking no notice of my invitation to come in, and threat to shoot him if he didn't. I would not have shot the brave fellow anyway, and I watched him walk deliberately back until he reached the works, when he leaped over them and ran for the woods like a deer. We concluded that he was a straggler who had been asleep somewhere, and did not know of the changed conditions, and thought his side still held the advanced line; at any rate, he found out the difference before it was too late.

Only a few moments elapsed before we were ready for the start, and away we went, expecting every minute the rebels would rise above their works, and put an end to us all. But all was quiet in front, so we kept on until we stood upon their works, and found that during the night the enemy had left for parts unknown. Upon a cracker box cover they had left the loving message,

"Come on, you damned Yanks to Richmond, but you will find it a rough road to travel, with a Hill, and two Longstreets to go over before you get there!"

You can imagine how surprised we were to find the works abandoned that our leaders had thought it impossible to capture by assault, and how thankful we were that we had not made the charge that the enemy had evidently expected, and so had prudently withdrawn, under cover of darkness. They had succeeded in removing their battery that had so raked us all day, but the heap of dead horses, a dozen or more, that lay near the position they had occupied, showed that they had made several attempts before they accomplished their purpose.

CHAPTER XX.

THE NORFOLK RAILROAD.

What wonder if the mouth is grim.
  That said so many swift "Goodbyes?"
Life's common words are idle breath,
  Beside those earnest battle cries.
What wonder if the gaze is dim,
  And yonder strangely lingers yet?
The eye that has looked straight at death,
  His image may not soon forget!

Unknown.

On the 12th of June, General Grant changed his plan of operations, and started us off for the James river. Our corps crossed the Chickahominy river at Long Bridge, marched southward to the James river, and on the 16th of June, the Army of the Potomac was on the right bank of the James, preparing for a fresh start in another direction. As we went up in front of Petersburg on the 18th of June, we were double quicked across an open field, and made a dash on the Norfolk railroad, where we made a stand.

It was in this charge that our beloved colonel, George L. Prescott, fell mortally wounded, while leading his men. He died the next day, and the whole brigade mourned his loss; he was a brave soldier, and a good man; always kind to his men, he treated them like brothers.

Many a time have I known him to let a sick man have his blanket, and then bunk in with a private who was lucky enough to have such an article. More than once has he slept with me, rolled up in the same blanket, and I always felt that in him I had a true friend. By his kind and generous words and deeds he had endeared himself to the whole brigade, and today many an old veteran reveres his memory, even as I do.

His body was brought home, and buried with his kindred in Sleepy Hollow cemetery, at Concord, Mass. I have visited his grave since the war, and as I stood in the pleasant spot where he sleeps so peacefully, I could but recall the memories of that terrible scene, when he laid his life on the altar of his country.

We had hot work all that day; again we charged the enemy, and drove them into their last line of works. This enabled us to establish our line on the crest of the hill. Near this place the mine was made that was exploded on the 30th of July, a little over a month later.

It was in this charge that a minie ball grazed my cheek, which soon swelled so that my comrades hardly recognized me. For a week or more, my jaw was rather stiff and sore, so that I could not eat hard bread; this made it rather inconvenient, as I was blessed with a good appetite and could not get much else but the old reliable "Hard tack" to eat, but I was not disabled, and did my duty as usual.

It was about noon, during a lull in the fight, that we saw a large turkey strut proudly into the centre of a deep ravine, that lay between us and the enemy's lines. Instantly every musket in our company was aimed at that poor turkey gobbler. When the smoke cleared away, we saw him still undisturbed in his foraging; we stood astonished until one of us happened to remember that our guns were sighted for 200 yards distance. He hastily lowered the sight, and spang went the deadly messenger into the heart of that devoted bird. When the fight was over, we picked up the fowl, and cooked him for our supper.

That night we spent in throwing up earthworks with our bayonets and tin plates, and by morning we had some works from which the enemy could not drive us, though they made several attempts. Our works were never advanced beyond this line until Petersburg was taken.

Chapter XXI.

EXTRACTS FROM MY DIARY.

Such is the price with which we bought
A country! And our sons here see
How faithfully the fathers wrought,
For manhood, peace, and liberty.

And you, ye sons, as here you tread,
And on our graves your tribute lay,
That ye be worthy of such dead,
Forget not till the latest day.

M. J. Savage.

June 1, 1864. Sunset. Another battle has begun, and brave men are now falling for their country and their homes. Ah, many a heart will mourn when they hear of this hour's history, but may the thought cheer them, that their dear ones fell like heroes, as they are, in the holiest cause for which man ever fought.

June 2. Five P. M. Again has the battle begun, and again we hear the hum of lead and iron, like hail in a storm. Oh, how terrible is the conflict of arms among men of one nation!

June 3. The battle began early this morning, and now many of my dear comrades are cold in death. Many others are suffering with pain from wounds received while facing traitors to their country.

At six o'clock this morning we charged across a field about a quarter of a mile; fighting began, and we had it hot and heavy until dark. Our loss was very heavy, and of my company, Warren P. Locke, and Makepeace C. Young are killed, and Hazen, Kennison, Robinson, Melvin, Parsons, Beals, Uffindale, and Fuller are wounded. Oh, may their names be ever honored by those who love their country!

June 4. Went out skirmishing; relieved at noon, and joined my company. Started for some place, and went about one mile, then back we went to the front, and staid all night.

June 5. Laid behind our works until four P. M., then with two other regiments, we went out on a reconnoisance; skirmishing began soon after starting, and we fell back to our works, got our rations, and fooled around all night.

June 13. Started at eight o'clock last night, and marched until half past four this morning, when we halted near the Chickahominy river; laid down an hour, then up and going again. Stopped for breakfast at seven o'clock. Crossed the Chickahominy, and went about a mile, then halted until dark; then packed up and started for Charles City courthouse. Stopped at midnight.

June 14. Once more back on the James river. I little thought one year ago that I should ever return here But where are my companions that were with me then? Some are lying beneath Virginia soil, others are wounded in the hospitals, and others are at home with their friends; but I am still in my country's service, fighting for the Nation that was given to us by our forefathers.

June 18. This day will ever be fresh in my memory, for through the mercy of God, my life was spared, when death certainly stared me in the face. While men fell all around me, I was left unharmed. It was a desperate attempt to carry the enemy's works; we charged three times and were repulsed each time, with terrible loss. Our Colonel fell, fatally wounded, while leading

his men in the charge. Major Edmunds was
wounded; William R. Wait was killed, and
Wheeler and many others of my company were
wounded.

June 19. Col. Prescott died of his wounds to-
day at 11 A. M. He was a good and brave man
and we deeply feel his loss.

July 30. Before Petersburg. Battle opened
all along the line before sunrise this morning.
About as heavy artillery firing as I ever heard.
There is hard fighting on the left and centre of
our line.

August 18. On guard last night; packed up
at three this morning, and moved to the left
across the Weldon railroad, and tore up the rails.
Heavy fighting all day; was on the skirmish line;
Melvin of my company wounded; was relieved
from the skirmish line at 10 o'clock tonight.

August 21. Sunday; on the Weldon railroad;
just got my breakfast down when the outposts of
our line were driven in; we opened fire, but were
driven back to our works, then we advanced,
skirmishing all the way back to our old picket
line.

CHAPTER XXII.

PETERSBURG.

"And this is what it means, to earn
  The title "Veteran" on a coat:
To march through flood and field, or lie
  Where rebel rifles sweep the moat;
To serve the guns in rifle pits;
  To sleep beneath the silent sky;
To dream of home, and wake to war;
  To see a comrade drop and die;
To hear and heed the fearful song
  Which whistling minnie bullets sing;
To faint and fall, and longing lie,
  For one cool draught from rocky spring."
Unknown.

After our line of entrenchments was established, our brigade was ordered to the rear, and we encamped along the Jerusalem plank road, where we were held in reserve for special duty. Here we worked day and night building a large earthen fort, which we named in honor of our lamented Col. Prescott. Here Major Edmunds was appointed colonel, and took command of the regiment.

We remained in reserve about three weeks, during which time we were called upon to re-enforce the Second and Sixth Corps, on two occasions. On July 12th we were ordered into the trenches, where we lived in bomb proofs for five weeks, one of the hardest experiences of my army life. These bomb proofs were a sort of artificial cavern, which we had to construct under cover of darkness, for the enemy was continually sending over to our lines solid shot and hissing shells, and only in our bomb proofs, (and not always there,) were we out of danger from them.

To build a bomb proof we dug a hole in the ground about four feet deep if the ground was dry, but where our regiment was located it was so springy that two feet brought us to water so most of ours were partly above ground; after the hole is dug, the top was roofed over with logs, and dirt thrown on top of them. A small space was left open towards our rear for a door to go in and out of, which was sheltered by a log canopy. Here we had to stay, and hot, uncomfortable, and unhealthy places they proved to be, and it is no wonder that many of our men were taken from them to the hospital, sick with malarial fever, from which some of them never recovered.

I remember one hot night, my chum and I pitched a tent two or three steps in the rear of our bomb proof under a pine tree, and there we went to sleep. Before morning, the active enemy in front began shelling our line, and we were awakened by the falling of the branches upon our tent, having been cut off by a passing shot. Soon another shot came and struck the tree, and my bedfellow made one leap out of the tent into the bomb proof. The next shot struck the tree still lower, and I too forsook my bed for the safer, though uncomfortable hole in the ground.

Sometimes, when the guns in front of us were silent, we would sit on the bomb proofs in the evening, and watch the shells of the enemy, as they came over on to some other part of our entrenchments. It was a beautiful sight, far beyond any fireworks I have ever witnessed, if we could only forget their deadly errand.

On the 30th of July occurred the explosion of the Burnside mine, that we had made by digging a passage to and under one of the rebel forts, and laying powder enough to destroy it. The plan had been carefully laid, and an attack contemplated simultaneous with the explosion, which would carry their line.

The blowing up of that mine was a horrible affair, and caused much slaughter, but for some reason, the attack was not a success. The artillery opened all along our line, on that eventful morning, as a signal for the beginning of the fight.

Near our bomb proof was a battery, which was so located that in firing, it would rake the rebel picket line on our left. The Captain of the battery knew that the first round would almost annihilate them, and wanted to give them a chance for their lives, so he wrote a note, telling them if they would leave their position and come over to us, they would save their lives; he then called for a volunteer to carry the note. Instantly a brave boy of our regiment stepped forward. He was told that it was a dangerous mission, and that he was risking his life, for he would certainly be shot at. His only reply was,

"Give me the message. I will go."

Holding up the white paper, he deliberately

walked across the open space to the rebel picket line, handed one of them the note, saying,

"Here you Johnnies, read that!"

He came back at the same moderate pace and strangely enough, was not shot at going or coming. All seemed astonished into silence at his daring, but he was loudly cheered, when he reached our line in safety.

The warning was in vain; the brave fellows would not desert their post, neither would they retreat without orders. Again came the order to rake their line; the order was obeyed, and two-thirds of the poor men were swept into eternity.

The captain of the battery was disgusted with such butchery. He could have fired on an advancing foe without scruple, but to fire on a thin picket line was too cold blooded for him, and he swore that he would not fire another shot in that direction, and he kept his word.

CHAPTER XXIII.

PEEBLE'S FARM.

"Forward——charge!
Into the smoke and hurling death,
Trampling friend and crushing foe;
Through the cannons' flaming breath,
Beneath the flag we rushing go."
Unknown.

On the 16th of August we were relieved from the trenches. on the 18th we made an attack on the Weldon railroad, in order to cut off the supplies of the rebel forces in front of Petersburg. In this action our regiment lost thirteen men. The railroad was too strongly guarded for our attempt to succeed.

We were called upon frequently to repel attacks from the enemy, and continually kept busy until the 1st of September, when we were

again ordered to the trenches for a few days.
We were soon relieved however, for our services
were required in another direction.

On the 30th of September the Fifth and
Ninth corps made a charge on the rebel Fort
Mc Rea. We formed our line in a piece of
woods, bringing the 32nd Massachusetts directly
in front of the fort, and the 4th Michigan on our
right. We had to cross an open field, and the
enemy's batteries opened on us directly, but we
went on steadily until we were in range of the
rebel rifles, then we made a dash, and soon reached the fort.

Our colonel received a wound in the leg,
and Col. Welch of the 4th Michigan fell mortally wounded. The first to mount the parapet was
an officer of our regiment; he jumped the deep
ditch in front of the fort, and swinging his sword
above his head, shouted to us to follow him; he
was followed by several officers, who jumped the
ditch and rushed into the fort. We soon followed them, though being encumbered with our
equipments, we could not as easily jump the
ditch as the officers. I jumped into the moat,
and shouted to a Johnny Reb to help me up the
slope; he shook his head, so I brought my gun to

my shoulder and threatened to shoot him. He reached out his hand and helped me up the bank.

Corporal Lewis Chesbro of my company, instead of climbing the bank, ran around to the rear of the fort, where he saw a rebel gunner sighting a piece of artillery towards a portion of our division that had not reached the works. Chesbro instantly shot the gunner, then tried in vain to turn the piece around. Seeing me inside the fort, he called for me to help him. Together we turned it partly round and sighted it at another of the rebel pieces of artillery, with which they were trying to escape.

The shot killed the two lead horses; the driver jumped down and cut the dead horses clear and managed to save the gun for us to face again the same day. After we had taken the first line of works, the Ninth corps passed to the front to take the second line. General Charles S. Griffin our commander, told us that we had done our duty well, and had done enough for one day, so we stacked arms and dropped down to rest.

Just at dusk, an aide came riding swiftly to our line, with the message that the left of the troops in front of us had broke, and our assistance was wanted. The order came clear and sharp:

"Fall in! Take arms! Left face! Forward double quick, march!"

General Griffin took the lead, shouting,

"Follow me!"

Away we went to where the troops had broke, and oh, what confusion! Shells bursting, men running here and there, every one for himself, and above all the noise was heard the rebel yell, once heard, never to be forgotten.

Our brigade passed through the retreating men, and began firing, to check if possible, the enemy's advance. This we did, and drove them back to their old position.

Here I saw a sight which in all the confusion and excitement thrilled me with admiration, something not often seen in action under any circumstances. The 155th Pennsylvania regiment of our brigade was on our right, firing by rank, and as cool as if on dress parade, and they continued so to do until we retired, leaving the recovered position for the Ninth corps to hold. Griffin's "Fighting brigade" was composed of seasoned veterans, and of them all, none were braver or bolder than the 155th Penn. volunteers.

Chapter XXIV.

WELDON RAILROAD.

The whizzing shell may burst in fire,
  The shrieking bullets fly
The heavens and earth may mingle grief,
  The gallant soldier die,
But while a haughty rebel stands,
  No peace! For peace is war.
The land that is not worth our death,
  Is not worth living for!

Unknown.

In October 1864, the re-enlisted men of the Ninth, Eighteenth, and Twenty-second Mass. Volunteers were transferred to our regiment, and we once more showed full ranks on parade. By a re-organization of our division, we were transferred to the Third brigade, now made up of veteran regiments and called the "Veteran Brigade."

As the weather grew colder, we went into winter quarters on the Jerusalem plank road, and built ourselves good log huts with chimneys, and proceeded to make ourselves comfortable, hoping we might be allowed to rest awhile.

But it was not to be, for on the 6th of December we had to leave our snug quarters and start off on the march, taking three days rations, and forty rounds of ammunition. We marched but three miles that day, and camped for the night by the roadside, not a very pleasant place on a cold winter's night.

Next day, after marching twelve miles, we found ourselves on the bank of the Nottoway river. We crossed it at midnight, and reached Sussex courthouse about daylight; stopped for breakfast, and after a short rest, resumed our march. At three o'clock in the afternoon we reached the Weldon railroad, about five miles from Jarrett's Station.

Here we began tearing up the rails, and destroyed the road for about fifteen miles We burned the sleepers, heated the rails in the flame, and twisted them all out of shape; some we wound around trees, and rendered them all completely useless. It was a long, hard job, and the second night found us bivouacked along the wrecked railroad.

On the 10th we started on our return to the front of Petersburg. Through snow and slush we marched twenty miles, stopping at night near Sussex courthouse. On this return march we had to live on the country, as we had taken but three days' rations, and were gone six days. Soon after starting we found three of our boys on the piazza of a house, with their throats cut. Apple jack was plenty, and they had probably drank too much and laid down, and were killed during their sleep.

We were wild with rage, and the murderers would have fared hard, had they fell into our hands. We buried our murdered comrades, and burned the house. We received orders to burn all the houses along the route except one, in which lived a well known Union man. Here I was left with a file of men as a safe guard until all our forces had passed. When we left, we received the heartfelt thanks of the women of the household.

On the 12th we again went into camp on the Jerusalem plank road, half a mile from our starting point. Here we again built our shanties, which we were allowed to consider as our homes for some time. The rest was very welcome, and it gave us time to write to our friends, and receive letters from home. I will close this chapter with an extract from my diary.

Dec. 18. The captain left for home on furlough. All the members of my company who did not re-enlist, were mustered out last month, and are now at home. How I would have liked to have gone with them! But I must wait, and hope there is a day coming when I too shall start for home.

Dec. 25. Christmas day. Letters and a diary from friends at home are very welcome. I have been very fortunate in receiving letters from home. The most cheering sound of all to us in camp is the bugle, "Fall in for the mail!" We promptly answer the summons, and eagerly listen as the orderly reads the names. Those who receive letters wander off by themselves to read them, those who receive newspapers share them with others, and still others gloomily stalk off, and wonder why the home-folks could not send at least one letter to cheer us on this dreary holiday. Ah, the time is never wasted, that is spent in writing to the soldiers at the front, assuring us that we are not forgotten in the homes to which we may never return. We cannot get too many letters, to help us fight the battles that must come before the war is over.

Dec. 31. On guard in a snow storm. One year ago I was on picket at Liberty, Va. What changes have taken place in one short year! Oh before the close of the next year, may this war be over, and myself, with all my brave comrades be at home with our friends. And now the year is gone with all its sorrow and care, never to return; but the memories connected with it can never die; they will ever bring to my mind many sorrows, and but few joys. So many of my dear companions in arms, who seemed like brothers, have been called to lay down their lives, but I have been spared in life and limb through the year that is past.

CHAPTER XXV

HATCHER'S RUN.

We know not what may be our lot,
  When future days have crowned us;
There's One above, whose arm of love,
  We hope may e'er surround us.

Goodbye! We go to meet the foe,
  The flag we love floats o'er us;
Its stars are bright, we'll win the fight,
  While treason falls before us.
Lilly Lovette.

New Years day 1865 found the 32nd Mass. living in their log huts on the Jerusalem plank road, one mile in rear of our line of works in front of Petersburg. Here we worked building and strengthening our works, taking turns so that the work went steadily on night and day. Thus we lived until late in the afternoon of Feb.

4th. when we received orders to move next morning at daybreak.

We imagined it was to be another railroad raid, and we left our huts standing, expecting to return to them; but in this we were mistaken. We started at daylight on the 5th, and marched all day, reaching Nottoway courthouse about sunset. Here we camped, and pickets were sent out, but were recalled at midnight, and we again took up our line of march, arriving early in the morning at a stream called Hatcher's run, at a point where it crossed the Vaughn road, and where the Second corps had fought the rebels the day before, while we were marching to re-enforce them.

We were ordered into some rifle-pits on the opposite side of the stream, out of which the enemy had been driven. I will try to describe my own experience in the battle that took place on February 6th, called by some historians the battle of Dabney's Mills, but known to us by the name of Hatcher's Run.

Our regiment was on the extreme right of the Fifth corps, connecting with the Second corps. About two o'clock in the afternoon, Crawford's division advanced from our left across our front and engaged the enemy. Two hours later the veteran brigade was called upon to fill a gap in Crawford's line.

We were in the rear, listening to the roar of battle, and pitying our comrades fighting so desperately in front of us, not knowing what moment our turn would come. General Warren sent an aid to General Griffin, our brigade commander, with orders to bring us to the front.

The bugle blew the fall-in call, and away we went into the storm of death. We marched left in front. When we reached the line engaged and passed through, the order came,

"File left! Right face!"
Bringing us into line of battle.

"Forward, double quick!"
On we went, not firing a shot. As our ranks were thinned by the sharp fire poured upon us,

"Close to the right!"
came the order, and we obeyed until we could go no farther, then came our turn, and we settled down to business.

The locality of the fight was in a grove of pines, where we could not see what was going on around us, and unknown to us, a fresh body of rebel troops drove back our main line of battle, and we were left alone. Before we fell back we saw a Johnnie Reb give a signal that he wanted to come into our lines; in he came, and informed us that,

"You uns will have to get out of this right smart, for they are putting the whole of Mahone's division in front and on the flanks of you uns!"
And in a short time I thought the whole rebel army was there!

Our little brigade was pushed back, fighting all the way, with heavy loss. Our regiment lost 74 men in killed, wounded, and missing. The 155th Pennsylvania was on our right, and that too lost heavily. Here Major Shepard was taken prisoner; the major, orderly of my company and myself were on the extreme right, and were so busily engaged that we did not notice that the line was falling back, until it was quite a distance from us. I informed the major, and when we three started to run, the rebs were not fifty feet away.

The major's scabbard tripped him and he fell; I looked back over my shoulder and saw a reb on each side of him, and knew he was a prisoner. This lent wings to my feet, and I expected every moment to feel a hand on my coat collar jerking me back, but I kept on, and the orderly and I reached the edge of the woods to find an attempt was being made to rally, in order to save an ammunition wagon from falling into the hands of the enemy.

But the attempt was a failure; it was nearly dark, and some of the new troops in the second line of battle, seeing us emerge from the woods, took us to be the Johnnies, and fired into us. At least half a dozen were killed or wounded by this volley, and this completed the disaster, for no troops, veteran or not, could be expected to rally when attacked on all sides, so we kept on until we reached our line of works.

Here we remained until the 11th, with the enemy's artillery making it very uncomfortable for us, then we moved to the rear about two miles, and camped for the night. Next day our tents and knapsacks came from our old camp, and we again began building our winter quarters. Here on the 18th of February as I was building a chimney to my shanty, I received a sergeant's warrant dated the 4th, and on the 20th I acted as sergeant of the guard for the first time.

On the 22nd we received orders to be ready to move at a moment's notice, and that no more furloughs were to be given, and everything looked as though another fight was at hand, but we remained here until the opening of the final campaign of the war.

CHAPTER XXVI.

ON FURLOUGH.

Home from the battlefield
For a brief rest;
Oh, what emotion fills
The soldier's breast.

Leaving his northern home,
Where all is peace,
Back to the battle-plain
'Till war shall cease.

L. M. J.

About the 18th of February I sent in an application for a furlough; I hardly expected to get it, as all furloughs had been refused, except in some cases, where an exceptional reason was urged, or strong influence brought to bear. I felt, after the hard experience of the past year, and with the prospect of another campaign full as hard, that a brief furlough was what I needed, so I could but try for one, which I did, and on Sunday the 26th of the same month, received a furlough for twenty days.

We had been paid off the day previous, and it did not take me long to prepare for the homeward trip. I said goodbye to my comrades and left for City Point that afternoon. None of the precious time must be wasted, so I made no stops on my journey home.

I left City Point on the morning of the 27th, on the steamer Daniel Webster, arriving at Fortress Munroe at four P. M., and an hour later left for Baltimore, arriving there at seven o'clock next morning; immediately left for New York, which place I reached at six o'clock that evening and took the train for home; traveled all night, and arrived at New Bedford on the morning of March 1st, where I was warmly welcomed by my friends.

Oh how pleasant seemed the dear old quiet city, after the terrible experience of the year that is past! And how quickly passed the time away! I paid a visit to my brother, now living in New Hampshire, and had a very enjoyable time. I spent the remainder of my time at home with my father, and among my friends, who could hardly do enough to make the time pass happily away.

Then too, I found that in the north, a soldier seemed to be considered of some account, and often strangers as they passed me in the street, had a pleasant word for the war-worn soldier in his faded suit of army blue.

All too soon the time arrived when I must bid my friends goodby. On the 16th of March I started for the front once more. I cannot dwell on the parting with my poor old father who seemed to feel that he would never see me again. But he was spared to welcome me home after the war was over, for which I still feel very thankful. It would have been a sad home-coming had he not been there to welcome me.

On my arrival in Boston, as I had a few hours to wait, I went to the State house to take a look at our old battle flag. What memories were awakened by that torn and smoky piece of silk, all that was left of the starry flag that I had followed for two long years. I felt sad at parting, "It might be for years, and it might be forever," and it was not a very cheerful journey back to the front. I reached my regiment on the 19th

of March, and received a warm welcome from
the boys of my company, and especially from my
tentmate. Dwight Graves, who prepared a good
supper of fried hardtack and pork in honor of
my arrival, and to which he, at least, did ample
justice.

I presented him with a piece of frosted
cake, sent him by a lady friend, which he considered a rare treat, and persisted in calling
"Wedding cake!" It took me several days to
settle down to army life, and army diet, but the
stern discipline and hard service soon brought
back my appetite, and my readiness to do whatever was required of me.

About eight o'clock in the morning of the
25th, we were ordered to fall in and move to the
right, for the enemy had attacked us in that
quarter; then moved to the left and attacked
them; hard fighting continued all day, without
food or rest. This fight was called the battle of
Fort Steadman.

We returned to camp about midnight,
where we remained until the 29th, when we
broke camp early in the morning, and marched
until noon. We stopped two hours for dinner
and rest, then started again, and went until five

P. M. Here we had another encounter with the enemy, and drove them some distance. We then moved to the front, and built works until midnight, and laid behind them until morning, when we again moved onward. I little thought as I slung my equipments and started on the march, that this was to be my last day of active service.

CHAPTER XXVII.

WOUNDED.

Upon that southern battle-field.
  One well remembered day.
I wore the loyal Union blue,
  And he, the rebel gray;
All day in conflict fierce and wild.
  Were mingled blue and gray,
And when night came, both he and I.
  Among the wounded lay,

L. M. J.

Our line of march led us in the direction of the Boydton plank road, and on the morning of March 30th the 32nd was detailed for the skirmish line. It was a rainy day, but we soldiers could not stop for the weather. About two o'clock in the afternoon, we sighted the enemy's pickets, and then firing began in earnest. All went well with me until about three o'clock, when I felt something strike my foot, not realizing that it was a bullet until I saw the jagged holes where it went in and out, breaking the bones as it went.

I stood and considered a moment whether to go to the rear or not, and finally decided to go back, get the surgeon to dress my wound, and then return to my company. It was quite a distance back to the rear, and I had to drop my gun and sit down to rest by the way. As I did so, I saw my colonel, who stopped and asked me if I was much hurt.

"Oh no," I replied, "Only slight, I will soon be back."

"I am glad it is no worse," he replied, and on he went.

I found the surgeon, had my foot bound up, and started to go back to my company.

"Where are you going?" asked the surgeon.

"Back to my company," said I.

"No you're not! Get on to that stretcher!" was the order, and I was obliged to obey, though I did not see the need of it; my foot did not pain me, only felt numb, and I felt a little weak and tired, which could hardly be wondered at. I was carried to the ambulance and taken to the field hospital, where I sat and waited for my turn to come. Meanwhile I saw such horrible wounds, that I can never forget or describe. It was a hard trial, for I was waiting for my turn to be operated upon, not knowing whether I would lose my foot or not.

My turn came at last, and I was given chloroform, and knew nothing more until I was being carried from the operating table to the hospital tent, when the rain beating on my face brought back my scattered senses.

Next morning the wounded were put on board box cars, and sent to City Point, arriving there late in the afternoon. Here I thought my journey was at an end, but I was mistaken once more.

The next morning the surgeon made his rounds at eight o'clock, and all the badly wounded were given a card, to show that they must be sent on board the steamer which was to start for Washington in an hour. I was pleased that I received no card, as it showed that I was not considered a bad case. At quarter to nine, the assistant surgeon came in.

"What sergeant, not on board yet?" Said he.

"No, I'm not going," I answered.

"We'll see about that!" he replied, and out he went. In a moment back he came with two men, who bundled me onto a stretcher and carried me on board the steamer just as she was to leave the dock.

We arrived in Washington on the morning of April 2nd and I was carried to Armory Square hospital, where I was bathed and put to bed. The lady nurse, a Miss Dixon of Connecticut, came with an orange and a glass of lemonade, but I could only shake my head in refusal, for I was in too much pain to speak. My foot had at last come to its feeling, and for the next twenty-four hours I suffered the most excruciating agony. I was given morphine, but it seemed to have no effect for a while.

The surgeons thought my foot would have to be taken off, but I begged them not to cripple me for life and they postponed the operation for a day. At their next visit, they decided the foot could be saved, and I was very thankful. I suffered a great deal after that, but my foot greatly improved, until finally on the 19th of April, I was allowed to get up, and managed to hobble on crutches down to ward I, to visit sergeant Buker.

Was up a few hours, then went to bed very tired and did not get up next day.

After that I was up every day, and soon was able to get round very well on crutches. I saw many sad sights during my stay in this hospital. Many a poor fellow gave up the weary struggle for life and died; one or two a day in my ward alone for sometime. We were treated very kindly, and received good care and nursing.

Many citizens visited the hospitals, and showed much sympathy for the sick and wounded veterans. There was an old colored woman who came daily with a big basket of pies, cakes, biscuits, and other good things, and her coming was always hailed with delight, for to those who were able to eat what she brought she gave liberally, and to those who could not, by order of the surgeons receive them, she gave kind cheering words promising to bring them something they could eat the next time she came.

I do not remember her name, only that we all called her "Aunty," and that her mistress allowed her to use all the time and material she desired to make these dainties for the sick men, who daily watched for her coming, and enjoyed the good things she brought. I can testify to

the fact that she was a good cook, and I shall
ever remember her with gratitude. The lady
nurses who cared so tenderly for the sick and
wounded soldiers, will ever be kindly remembered by me.

Meanwhile stirring events were taking
place. Lee's surrender, which ended the fighting, and the assassination of President Lincoln
occurred while I lay helpless in the hospital.
How I longed to be up and about, to help finish
the work in which I had been so long engaged.

After the surrender of Lee, and the succeeding events, the army was massed around
Washington, my regiment with the rest, and my
tentmate Graves, and several other comrades
came to see me, and it was from them that I
learned what took place after I was wounded.

CHAPTER XXVIII.

CLOSING SCENES.

They yield, they turn, they fly the field.
 We smite them as they run;
Their arms, their colors are our spoil,
 The furious fight is done!
Across the plain we follow far,
 And backward push the fray;
Cheer! Cheer! The grand old army
 At last has won the day!

Stedman.

I can give the further movements of my regiment after I was wounded, only from what I learned later from my comrades, for to my great regret, I was not with them to the end. The Fifth corps kept on in spite of the enemy's artillery, until they reached around the extreme right of the confederate line of works in front of

Petersburg. Next day they were relieved by the Second corps, and moved off again to the left, a little to the west of the Boydton road. Here they were attacked, and driven back, but again advanced and drove the rebels back.

Four companies of our regiment were in the line of skirmishers, and seized the opportunity to get in the rear of the rebel skirmishers, who were so surprised that they hastily retreated leaving their dinner and stacked arms, all of which were confiscated by the boys of the 32nd. We were now on the extreme left of our army and towards night our brigade was sent out to find, and if possible to re-enforce General Sheridan. We had all we could attend to in driving the enemy out of our way, and it was morning before we reached Sheridan.

That day, April 1st, was fought the battle of Five Forks by the Fifth corps and the cavalry, all under the command of the dashing and dauntless Phil Sheridan. It was a complete victory for our side, and we captured five thousand prisoners.

Next day, by order of General Sheridan, General Warren was relieved of the command of the Fifth corps, and our brigade commander,

General Griffin took his place. The colonel of our regiment, James A. Cunningham was placed in command of a brigade of skirmishers, and Ambrose Bancroft, captain of our company, (B.) was placed in command of the 32nd, which was included in Cunningham's brigade.

Next day we were deployed to the west, and reaching the South Side railroad, captured a train of sick and wounded soldiers, took many other prisoners, and a great quantity of stores and supplies. Here we learned that General Lee was leaving Petersburg, and retreating southward, and General Sheridan hastened with his cavalry and the Fifth corps to cut off his retreat.

On the 4th of April we seized the only railroad by which Lee could escape, and on Sunday, the 9th, he made a final attempt to cut his way through our cavalry's lines. Our brigade had marched all day and half the night, and enjoyed about two hours rest, when we were called upon to re-enforce the cavalry.

Away we went, the 32nd leading the column, the men gay and bright, and their guns glistening in the sunshine. At the sight of our coming the enemy retreated; they had no desire to encounter the "Fighting Fifth" that day.

Soon we received the order "Forward." We advanced under a sharp fire from their artillery, and their front line fell back from our attack. Just then General Lee sent one of his staff with a flag of truce, and all hostilities ceased.

We soon heard that General Grant and General Lee were holding a conference, and at four P. M. the general orders announced that Lee had surrendered. How profound was our emotion when we realized that the war was at an end!

The following day the two armies were mingled together like old friends. The brave confederates were entirely destitute of rations, and we shared ours with the half starved men, who had fought so long and so desperately for a cause that was lost. The next day was the formal surrender of arms. Our brigade received the surrender, and the 32nd was on the right of the line. Drawn up in line of battle, guns at shoulder, loaded and capped, eyes front, no cheering, no jeering, only a sympathetic silence, while the gallant but defeated foe advanced in front the length of our line, then faced us, stacked arms, laid colors and equipments on stack, then marched away to make room for another line.

until all had given up their arms. It was a thrilling sight, never to be forgotten by those who witnessed it.

After the surrender the regiment was kept busy in various ways, but at last started for Washington in time to take part in the grand review, which occurred on the 23rd and 24th of May, 1865. I could not march with my comrades, but witnessed the parade from a stand reserved for disabled veterans. In those two days, 150 000 men marched up Pennsylvania Avenue from the Capitol, by the White House, out to Georgetown, and across the Potomac river into Virginia once more.

What a sight it was! I cannot describe my feelings as I saw those columns of veterans march by, knowing so well what they had endured, and what they had accomplished. I was proud to call them comrades. Nor did I forget the many thousands of brave men who died that their country might live. I thought sadly of my companions in arms, whose faces I missed when my regiment passed by; they will never be forgotten until I too have joined the grand army of the dead.

CHAPTER XXIX.

MUSTERED OUT.

They are coming from the wars,
They are bringing home their scars,
They are bringing back the old flag too in glory:
They have battled long and well,
And let after ages tell,
How they won the proudest name in song or story.

Eugene H. Munday.

I remained in Armory Square hospital until the 26th of May, when I was transferred to a place called White Hall, on the Delaware river, about eighteen miles above Philadelphia. It was formally a seminary, but had been taken for hospital use. At the time I wished it had always remained what it was built for, as it was the most lonesome and dreary place I ever saw. The

nearest place was a village called Bristol, two
miles away, and we went there when we could,
and those who were able traveled the country for
miles around, just to pass the time away. It
seemed very hard, now that the war was over,
and our services no longer needed, that we could
not return to our homes.

On the 7th of June they began mustering
out men of the different states, and fifty to a
hundred men left the hospital for home every
day. Day after day passed, and there still remained all those of my regiment, six or seven,
with no sign of being mustered out.

On the 3rd day of July we heard of our
regiment passing through Philadelphia on its way
home, and then we could content ourselves no
longer. We wanted to be with them when they
entered old Massachusetts again, and to be with
our comrades once more before the regiment was
disbanded, and those who had been our companions so long were scattered far and wide.

We went to the surgeon in charge, and
asked him why we were not discharged.

"It takes a long while to get your descriptive
lists from the front, and I intend to have you
veterans discharged for wounds received in ac-

tion, and you would get a hundred dollars extra," was his reply.

But that was no inducement to me to stay there any longer, and I asked him if I could not be sent to my regiment, and he gave his consent, so on the 6th of July, in company with one or two others of my regiment, I bade goodbye to my hospital life, and started for Massachusetts.

Arriving in Boston on the evening of the 7th, we remained there that night and the next morning took the steamer for Galloupe's Island, where our regiment was quartered.

Here we remained until the thirteenth, when the regiment was disbanded, and the boys left for their homes. The 32nd was no more, but their deeds will never die.

I went back to Boston to wait for my discharge, made a brief visit home to spend Sunday and returned to Boston, where on the 18th of July 1865, I received my discharge, and was a free man once more, having served Uncle Sam for three years, eight months and sixteen days. I was with my company from the time I enlisted until I was wounded, with the exception of two furloughs. My wound was healed, though I had to use a cane for some time longer.

When I enlisted, my mind was made up to do my duty, whatever the consequences, and I trust it will not seem like boasting when I say that I did so every time. When traitors tried to destroy the best government that ever existed, and dishonor their country's flag, I felt it was my duty to enlist and do what I could for my native land, and I have never been sorry that I did so.

My health was always good, and I was fortunate in battle, never being laid off duty until I was wounded, just before the last battle in which my regiment participated. In thirty-eight battles, I shared the dangers with my comrades of company B. But where are the 101 men of my company who left Concord for Fort Warren on that cold morning of December 3rd, 1861? I called the roll of company B in 1865, when there were but eight men left of the original company.

Ah, the memories that arise of the brave boys who shared with me the hardships and dangers of those long years of warfare! Brothers could not be dearer than those who have shared their last hardtack with me, helped me off the field when wounded, cheered me on the long and tiresome march when I was about ready to give up and drop by the wayside. I think I used to dread the long marches more than I did the battles, and welcome the sight of a brush with the enemy that would stop the march for a while.

We had each to carry a musket, 40 to 80 rounds of ammunition, haversack with four to six days rations, knapsack, blanket, shelter tent, together with our canteen and other small articles that we could not do without, and to carry this on the march from ten to twenty hours at a time with only a few moments now and then to rest, often seemed more of a trial to me than the hardest fought battle I was ever in.

But the hardest trial of all was to have my comrades shot down on my right and on my left, and have to rush on with the rest in the charge, or in battle, leaving them behind to suffer and die.

No words can do justice to that experience, or the feeling of the battle-worn soldier, when he starts out after the battle is over to hunt up his comrades that have not answered the roll-call, will never answer it again, and he digs a hole in the ground with his bayonet and wrapping a blanket around his dead comrade's body, lays him to rest in an unknown grave forevermore.

And now my story is told; it is a plain, true tale of my experience in the War of the Rebellion, and may help the future generations to understand just what their fathers suffered, that their native land might remain forever, an undivided nation.

CONTENTS.

CHAP.   PAGE.

I	ENLISTMENT	1
II	TO THE SEAT OF WAR	6
III	ON THE MARCH	10
IV	ANTIETAM	14
V	UNDER ARREST	17
VI	IN CAMP	21
VII	FREDERICKSBURG	25
VIII	CHANCELORSVILLE	29
IX	BRANDY STATION & ALDIE	33
X	GETTYSBURG	38
XI	MINE RUN	44
XII	A LETTER FROM THE FRONT	48
XIII	RE-ENLISTED	52
XIV	AT HOME AGAIN	55
XV	IN THE WILDERNESS	59
XVI	LAUREL HILL	63
XVII	WILDERNESS CAMPAIGN	69
XVIII	LEAVES FROM MY DIARY	73
XIX	COLD HARBOR	79
XX	NORFOLK RAILROAD	85

Contents.

XXI	EXTRACTS FROM MY DIARY	88
XXII	PETERSBURG	92
XXIII	PEEBLE'S FARM	97
XXIV	WELDON RAILROAD	101
XXV	HATCHER'S RUN	106
XXVI	ON FURLOUGH	112
XXVII	WOUNDED	117
XXVIII	CLOSING SCENES	123
XXIX	MUSTERED OUT	128